I0563809

Junius Davis

Alfred Moore and James Iredell
Revolutionary patriots, and associate justices of the Supreme Court of the United States. An address delivered in presenting their portraits to the Supreme Court of North Carolina on behalf of the North Carolina Societ

ISBN/EAN: 9783337235505

Printed in Europe, USA, Canada, Australia, Japan

Cover: Foto ©Andreas Hilbeck / pixelio.de

More available books at **www.hansebooks.com**

Junius Davis

Alfred Moore and James Iredell

Revolutionary patriots, and associate justices of the Supreme Court of the

United States. An address delivered in presenting their portraits to the

Supreme Court of North Carolina on behalf of the North Carolina Societ

THE

STATE OF THE DEPARTED,

SET FORTH IN

A FUNERAL ADDRESS,

DELIVERED AT THE INTERMENT

OF THE

RIGHT REV. BENJAMIN MOORE, D. D.

Bishop of the Protestant Episcopal Church in the State of New-York, and Rector of
Trinity Church, in the City of New-York,

On Friday, the first Day of March, 1816, in Trinity Church,
in the City of New-York;

AND

A DISSERTATION

ON THE SAME SUBJECT.

———◆———

BY JOHN HENRY HOBART, D. D.

Bishop of the Protestant Episcopal Church in the State of New-York.

———◆———

THIRD EDITION.

NEW-YORK:

PRINTED BY T. AND J. SWORDS,
No. 99 Pearl-street.

1825.

STATE OF THE DEPARTED,

A FUNERAL ADDRESS,

&c. &c.

PEOPLE of the congregation! the remains of your Pastor lie before you—the beloved Pastor who so long fed you with the bread of life, and whose accents of persuasion you have so often heard in this sacred place.

My brethren of the Episcopal clergy! we have long mourned the living death of our spiritual Father —his sufferings are terminated—he is at rest.

When we contemplate that venerated corpse, it is natural to inquire,

What has become of the spirit which so recently inhabited it?

What will become of that tabernacle of clay which this spirit has deserted?

Christian believers, these are inquiries deeply interesting to you. Soon each one of you will be, as he whose remains you now behold.

What becomes of the spirit of the believer when it leaves its tabernacle of clay?

Does it sink into annihilation? We must subdue all those feelings which constitute the perfection and happiness of our nature, before we can contemplate the extinction of being but with horror. There is not a power of his soul which man does not shudder at the thought of losing—not a virtuous enjoyment which he does not wish to carry with him beyond the grave —not an acquisition that ennobles or adorns him which he would not impress with the seal of eternity. The voice of the Creator speaks in the soul of the being whom he has made, and inspires the hope that he is immortal. But, alas! that voice is only faint and feeble. Immortality, an unmerited gift to a fallen creature, must be assured by the express promise of him who alone can bestow it. The word of the Author of our being must be the pledge, that this being shall not be extinguished.

Blessed be God—this word we have—God hath spoken—" The spirit shall return to him who gave it."

This, believer, is thy confidence and thy rejoicing. Thy spirit returns to God—to God all glorious and all good; who so loved thee as to give for thee his only begotten Son; and who in the blood of his Son hath sealed the assurance that thou shalt be ever with him. Canst thou doubt whether in his presence thou shalt be happy? Ah! the happiness reserved for thee by thy God, thine eye hath not seen, thine ear hath not heard, and thy heart cannot conceive. But,

When does the spirit enter on this state of complete felicity?

There cannot be a moment's doubt, that departed saints do not enter on the *full* fruition of bliss immediately on their release from the body. In what does this fulness of bliss consist? In the union of the purified spirit with the glorified body. But until the voice of the Son of God calls to the corruptible to put on incorruption, and the mortal immortality, that body is confined to the tomb, embraced by corruption, mingled with the dust. Admission to heaven, the place of the vast universe of God, where the vision of his glory, more immediately displayed, shall constitute the eternal felicity of the redeemed, does not take place, according to the sacred writings, until the judgment at the great day; when the body, raised incorruptible and glorious, shall be united to the soul, purified and happy. While the soul is separate from the body, and absent from that heaven which is to be her eternal abode, she cannot have attained the perfection of her bliss.

Will the privileges of believers be greater than those of their divine Head? His glory in heaven consists in the exaltation of his human nature—of his glorified

body in union with his perfect spirit. But in the
interval between his death and his resurrection, his
body was embalmed by his disciples, washed with
their tears, and guarded in the sepulchre by his enemies.
His spirit therefore was not in heaven until he ascended
there after his resurrection. " Touch me not," said
he to Mary Magdalene, when he had risen from the
dead, " for I have not yet ascended to your Father
" and my Father, to your God and my God."*   Our
blessed Lord, in his human nature, was not in heaven
until after his resurrection. And will a privilege be
conferred on the members which was not enjoyed by
the Head?   " This day thou shalt be with me in
" Paradise," was his language to the penitent thief
associated with him at his crucifixion—in Paradise, not
in heaven; for the happiness of heaven supposes the
happiness of the whole man, of his soul united to his
body. But on that day in which the Saviour assured
the penitent subject of his mercy that he should be
with him in Paradise, the body of the one was con-
signed to corruption, and the body of the other to the
tomb.

What then is the state of the soul in the period
between death and the resurrection—between her separation from the body and her re-union with it—between her release from this her state of exile, and her
admission to final and complete felicity in her eternal
home?

* John xx. 17.

Is she in a state of unconsciousness? All probability is against the supposition. Consciousness
seems a necessary attribute of spirit in a disembodied
state. The temporary suspension of consciousness in
the present life arises from that union of the soul with
the body, which in many cases controls, and changes,
and suspends her operations.

But a state of unconsciousness is a state of oblivion
—and this must be an object of aversion to the happy
spirit. In the present life indeed there is often an
oblivion of care that corrodes, of adversity that wounds
the spirit—or that which, from the connexion of the
body with the soul, is necessary to the renewed exer-
tion of its powers, and to renewed enjoyment. But
when the soul, with her mortal tabernacle, has shaken
off her sins and sorrows, this oblivion cannot be necessary; it must interrupt her enjoyment—it cannot therefore be assigned her in a state which, her probation
being finished, is a state of reward and of bliss.

But, on this as on every other point connected with
our spiritual interests, we are not left to speculation,
and to a balance of probabilities. What was the language of our blessed Lord to his penitent companion
on the cross?—" This day thou shalt be with me in
" Paradise." But would this have been the language
of consolation, of hope, of triumph, if Paradise be a
state of oblivion? Or can we for a moment indulge
the idea, that the human soul of the blessed Jesus, sunk
at death into a state of forgetfulness, which reduced it
to a level with the body that was sleeping in the sepulchre? No; his soul was actively engaged—engaged

in prosecuting that gracious scheme of redemption
which occupied his life, which engrossed his last mo-
ments of agony, and which he relinquished not even
with death. He "went," says the apostle,* "and
"preached to the spirits in prison," to the spirits in safe
keeping, "to the *sometime* disobedient," but finally
penitent antediluvians, "in the days of Noah," who,
though they were swept off in the deluge of waters,
found, through the merits of the Lamb slain from the
beginning of the world, a refuge from the flames of
Tophet, from the surges of the burning lake. While
his body was reposing in the grave, he went in his
spirit and "preached," or (as the word signifies) *proclaimed*, the glad tidings, to the souls of the departed
saints, of that victory over death which the Messiah, in
whom they trusted, was to achieve; and of that final
redemption of the body and resurrection to glory, the
hope of which constituted their enjoyment in the place
of the departed.†

* 1 Peter iii. 19, 20.

† The above is the interpretation of this very obscure passage,
which is advanced and maintained with great ingenuity, force,
and erudition, by Bishop Horsley, in his Sermon on "Christ's
"descent into Hell." This interpretation gives no sanction, as
Bishop Horsley justly observes, to the doctrine of purgatory.
Purgatory is considered as a place of punishment and purification
for those who die under the guilt of sins of infirmity, from which
they are delivered either when they have been sufficiently purified
by suffering purgatorial pains, or by the efficacy of the masses
which are said for them. There is no foundation for this doctrine
in Scripture. At death the souls of the righteous and of the
wicked go to a state, the one of happiness, and the other of misery,
in the place of the departed; and there is no *change* in their state

Could God, who is "the God of the living" only, be styled emphatically "the God of Abraham, of Isaac, "and of Jacob," if their departed spirits did not live to him in a state of consciousness and enjoyment?[*] Did the holy apostle, who in labours and in sufferings died daily, and who daily was renewed by the hope of the glory prepared for him, look forward to a state of unconsciousness after death, when he desired to "de-

except what arises from the complete consummation, in *body* as well as soul, of the happiness of the one in Heaven, and the misery of the other in (γέεννα) Hell.

Christ proclaimed, to the spirits in prison, in a state of seclusion and separation, or, as the word may be translated, in *safe keeping*, the glad tidings of his victory over death, of their final resurrection to glory. Were they previously in doubt as to these events—a doubt which must have been incompatible with their happiness? By no means. They died in the faith that the Messiah was to achieve this victory; and in this faith their spirits rejoiced. But Christ, when he descended to them, changed their faith in this event as *future*, into faith in it as actually *accomplished*—and he thus *confirmed* the glorious hopes which they *already enjoyed*.

But why are the antediluvians, those who were "*sometime* dis-"obedient," but afterwards became penitent "in the days of "Noah," selected as the peculiar objects of the Saviour's preach ing? "To this I can only answer," (says Bishop Horsley,) "that I think I have observed in some parts of Scripture an "anxiety, if the expression may be allowed, to convey distinct "intimations, that the antediluvian soul is not uninterested in the "redemption and the final retribution."

But for full answer on this point, and on many other inquiries connected with this subject, the reader is referred to Bishop Horsley's Sermon on Christ's descent into Hell, published at the end of his new translation of Hosea, and in the volumes of his sermons.

[*] Matt. xxii. 32.

" part and to be with Christ," to be " absent from the
" body and present with the Lord?"

No—believer, when thy soul departs from the body,
she does not pass into that state of utter forgetfulness,
which, even in the present scene of sin and woe, thou
dost dread as the greatest evil with which thou canst
be visited.   Thou wilt go to a place of enjoyment—
characterized as the *bosom of Abraham;* because there
thou wilt be blessed with the company of this Father
of the Faithful, of patriarchs and prophets, who are
all waiting their consummation, the redemption of the
body.   Thou wilt go to *Paradise*—to that place separate and invisible—but where thou shalt be with Christ,
and be present with the Lord; anticipating in constant
desire, in rapturous hope, the resurrection at the last
day.   Then he who holds the keys of death and hell
shall say to thy spirit—Go forth—be clothed upon
with an house that is from heaven; enter into the joy
of thy Lord; inherit a kingdom prepared for thee from
the foundation of the world.

Yes—my fellow Christians—this is the joyful confidence with which we can meet the interesting inquiry—

What will become of the body when it is deserted
by the spirit that animates it?

What can reason teach us here?   She may indeed
by analogy illustrate and confirm the doctrine of the
resurrection when it is revealed—but as an original
truth, she knew nothing of it.   The tomb received, in

its dark embrace, the mouldering body; and there was no light that dawned on the night of the grave. " Blessed then. be the God and Father of our Lord " and Saviour Jesus Christ, who hath begotten us to " a lively hope by the resurrection of Jesus Christ from " the dead."* He is " the first fruits of them that " slept"†—and at the great harvest at the last day, " those who sleep in Jesus will God bring with him."‡ —The body, sown in corruption, shall be raised in incorruption—sown in dishonour, it shall be raised in glory—sown in weakness, it shall be raised in power— sown a natural body, it shall be raised a spiritual body.—Blessed, blessed be the God and Father of our Lord Jesus Christ, who hath begotten us to this lively hope by the resurrection of Jesus Christ from the dead.

How is all this to be effected? By that mighty power which raised up Christ from the dead. Here we take our stand—on the omnipotence of God—and defy every attack against the doctrine of the resurrection. We laugh to scorn all attempts to wrest from us our hope, through a supposed impossibility of the resurrection, as puny struggles against the omnipotence of God. Did he not at first construct a human form from the dust of the earth? Did he not breathe into a mass of clay the breath of life? And when he again speaks, shall it not be done? Can he not again bring bone to its bone, sinew to its sinew, flesh to its flesh? Fear not, Christian! thy dust may be scattered to the

---

* 1 Pet. i. 3.   † 1 Cor. xv. 20.   ‡ 1 Thess. iv. 14

winds of heaven—But thy God is there. It may repose in the lowest abysses of the grave—He is there.
It may dwell in the uttermost parts of the sea—Even
there his hand shall lead thee, his right hand shall hold
thee, and bring thee forth, incorruptible and glorious,
like unto that body which now receives the homage
of the angels around the throne. Fear not—thy Redeemer is almighty; and thou shalt be raised at the
last day.

Let us comfort one another with these words—

Our venerable Father has gone. In the bosom of
Abraham, in the paradise of God, in the custody of
the Lord Jesus, his soul reposes; waiting in peace
and joy its " perfect consummation and bliss in God's
" eternal and everlasting glory." Soon the sentence
that sin has brought on the whole human race is to
be pronounced on the revered remains before us—
" Earth to earth—ashes to ashes—dust to dust."

But, he lives with us in the memory of his virtues.
Let us recall and cherish them. Let us keep him a
little longer with us—not as of late when languishing
under disease he gradually lost that engaging expression which had so eminently characterized him, until
he at last sunk in the darkness of death—But let us
view him such as you, people of the congregation,
beheld him, when he appeared among you as your
Pastor—such as we, my brethren, beheld him, when
he exercised over us his paternal authority.

I should indeed violate that simplicity which in a
high degree adorned him, if I were to indulge in the
language of inflated panegyrick. Simplicity was his

distinguishing virtue. He was unaffected—in his tempers, in his actions, in every look and gesture. Simplicity, which throws such a charm over talents, such a lustre over station, and even a celestial loveliness over piety itself, gave its insinuating colouring to the talents, the station, and the piety, of our venerable Father. But it was a simplicity accompanied with uniform prudence, and with an accurate knowledge of human nature.

A grace allied to simplicity, was the meekness that adorned him—a meekness which was " not easily " provoked"—never made an oppressive display of talents, of learning, or of station—and condescended to the most ignorant and humble, and won their confidence; while associated with dignity, it commanded respect and excited affection, in the circles of rank and affluence. And it was a meekness that pursued the dictates of duty, with firmness and perseverance.

His piety arising from a lively faith in the Redeemer whom he served, and whose grace he was commissioned to deliver, warmed as it was by his feelings, was ever under the control of sober judgment. A strong evidence of its sincerity was, its entire freedom from every thing like ostentation. It did not proclaim itself at the corners of the streets—it did not make boastful pretensions, or obtrude itself on the public gaze—but it was displayed in every domestic, every social, every public relation. It was not the irregular meteor, glittering for a moment, and then sinking in the darkness, from which it was elicited; but the

serene and steady light that shineth more and more
unto the perfect day.

He rose to public confidence and respect, and to
general esteem, solely by the force of talents and
worth.   In the retirement of a country village, the
place of his nativity, he commenced his literary career,
and he prosecuted it in the public seminary of this
city, and subsequently in his private studies, until he
became the finished scholar, and the well furnished
divine.

This city was the only scene of his parochial labours.
Here he commenced, and here he has closed his minis-
terial life.*

* Bishop Moore was born October 5, 1748, at Newtown, Long-
Island. He went to school in Newtown, and afterwards in New-
York, in order to prepare for entering King's (now Columbia)
College, where he graduated.

He pursued his studies, after he graduated, at Newtown, under
the direction of Dr. Auchmuty, Rector of Trinity Church; and
he was engaged some years in teaching Latin and Greek to the
sons of several gentlemen in New-York.

He went to England in May, 1774; was ordained *Deacon,*
Friday, June 24, 1774, in the chapel of the Episcopal palace at
Fulham, by Richard Terrick, Bishop of London, and *Priest,*
Wednesday, June 29, 1774, in the same place, by the same
Bishop.

After his return from England he officiated in Trinity Church
and its chapels, and was appointed, with the Rev. Mr. Bowden,
(now Dr. Bowden, of Columbia College) an Assistant Minister of
Trinity Church; Dr. Auchmuty being Rector, and afterwards
Dr. Inglis, since Bishop of Nova-Scotia.

On the resignation of Bishop Provoost, Dr. Moore was appointed Rector of Trinity Church, December 22, 1800. He was

People of the congregation! you have seen him, regular and fervent, yet modest and humble, in performing the services of the sanctuary. You cannot have forgotten that voice of sweetness, and of melody, yet of gravity and solemnity, with which he excited while he chastened your devotions; nor that evangelical eloquence which, gentle as the dew of Hermon, insinuated itself into your hearts.

His love for the Church was the paramount principle that animated him. He entered on her service in the time of trouble. Steady in his principles, yet mild and prudent in advocating them, while he never sacrificed consistency, he never provoked resentment. In proportion as adversity pressed upon the Church, was the firmness of the affection with which he clung to her. And he lived until he saw her, in no inconsiderable degree by his counsel and exertions, raised from

unanimously elected Bishop of the Protestant Episcopal Church in the State of New-York, at a special Convention, in the city of New-York, September 5, 1801; and was consecrated Bishop at Trenton, New-Jersey, in St. Michael's Church, Friday, September 11, 1801, by the Right Rev. Bishop White, of Pennsylvania, Presiding Bishop; the Right Rev. Bishop Clagget, of Maryland; and the Right Rev. Bishop Jarvis, of Connecticut.

He was attacked by a paralysis, in February, 1811; and for the last two or three years repeated attacks gradually weakened and disabled him, until he expired, at his residence at Greenwich, near New-York, on Tuesday evening, the 27th of February, 1816, in the 60th year of his age. The duties of the Episcopal office in this diocese have been discharged by the author of this address as Assistant Bishop, since his consecration, in May, 1811. [1816. And after the decease of Bishop Moore he became the sole Bishop of the diocese.]

the dust, and putting on the garments of glory and beauty.

It was this affection for the Church which animated his Episcopal labours—which led him to leave that family whom he so tenderly loved, and that retirement which was so dear to him, and where he found, while he conferred enjoyment, and to seek in remote parts of the diocese for the sheep of Christ's fold. I know that his memory lives where I have traced the fruits of his labours.

My brethern of the Episcopal clergy! I need not tell you how much prudence, gentleness, and affection, distinguished his Episcopal relation to you.

We are not without many recent monitions of that summons which we shall all receive—Give an account of thy stewardship. A Presbyter whose worth and usefulness, from his vicinity to us, are well known, has been recently taken from us.* But a few months since, and this temple witnessed your attendance on the last solemn offices of a venerable Father.† The remains of another are now before us. With the exception of one,‡ to whom we still look with reverence, who was the companion of his youth, the associate of his early labours, and the sympathizing friend of his old age, he is the last in this diocese of those venerable men who derived their ordination from the Parent Church, and whose characters are marked by attachment to evangelical truth in connexion with primitive

* The Rev. Elias Cooper, Rector of St. John's Church, Yonkers.
† The Right Rev. Bishop Provoost.
‡ The Rev. Dr. Bowden.

order. My brethren—let not their principles descend with them to the grave. Soon our course will be finished; our account will at the great day be demand· ed; and how awful the responsibility of those to whom Christ hath intrusted the charge of " the sheep for " whom he shed his blood, of the congregation which " is his spouse and body."

People whom I see before me! you have an account to render—an account of the use which you have made of your talents, your time, your privileges; of the means of grace and salvation. Animating is the re-flection that to the servant who faithfully employs the talents intrusted to him, there is a *resurrection of life.* But let us remember—Blessed Jesus—let us remem-ber, and by a living faith lay hold on thee as our refuge—thou hast declared, there is the *resurrection of damnation.*

DISSERTATION

ON THE

STATE OF DEPARTED SPIRITS,

AND THE

DESCENT OF CHRIST INTO HELL.

———◆———

THE author of the preceding address having been naturally led, in the consideration of the inquiry concerning the condition of the soul after its departure from the body, to introduce the doctrine of a separate state between death and the resurrection, it seems proper more fully to explain and establish the sentiments advanced on this subject.

He has reason to believe that the doctrine is not generally understood; and that, therefore, it is regarded by many as a doctrine of little importance, and of curious speculation only; and, by others, as a dangerous novelty, nearly allied to the tenets concerning purgatory held by the Church of Rome.

It shall therefore be its object to show,

I. That it is a doctrine of the Church of England, and of the Protestant Episcopal Church.

II. That it may be traced to the apostolic age. And,

III. That it is clearly revealed in the sacred writings.

The doctrine is—that the souls of men do not go immediately to *Heaven*, the place of final bliss, nor to *Hell*, the place of final torment, but remain in a state of enjoyment or misery in the place of the departed,* until the resurrection at the last day; when, their bodies being united to their souls, they are advanced to complete felicity or woe in Heaven or Hell.†

I. This is a doctrine of the Church of England, and of the Protestant Episcopal Church.

In the rubric before the Apostles' Creed, in the American Liturgy, it is stated that the words, " He " went into the *place of departed spirits*," are considered as words of the same meaning with " He de- " scended into *Hell*."

In the prayer for Christ's Church militant in the communion service, we are taught to beseech God that " we, with all those who have departed this life in " his faith and fear, *may* be partakers of his heavenly " kingdom." The happiness of heaven is here considered as a future event in respect to those departed, as well as to ourselves.

In like manner, in the prayers of the burial service, we beseech Almighty God that "we, with all those " who are departed in the true faith of his holy name, " may have our *perfect consummation and bliss both* " *in body and soul*, in his eternal and everlasting

* Styled in the New Testament ᾅδης, hades, or *Hell;* in the sense of an invisible place.

† Styled γίεννα, gehenna, also in the New Testament translated *Hell*, denoting a place of torment.

glory." The faithful who are departed have not *yet* their perfect consummation and bliss both in body and soul.

II. This doctrine has been maintained by a series of Protestant divines eminent for learning and piety, and may be traced to the apostolic age.

Dr. Campbell, of the *Presbyterian* Church of Scotland, and formerly Principal of Marischal College, Aberdeen, in a very learned dissertation prefixed to his " translation of the four gospels," on the words " ᾅδης and γίεννα," maintains and vindicates this doctrine of an intermediate state. His arguments on this point are full, clear, forcible, and conclusive.

Dr. Macknight, of the same Church, the author of a *Harmony of the Gospels*, and of a *New Translation of the Epistles, with a Commentary and Notes*, in various parts of the latter work maintains, that the righteous do not enter on the bliss of Heaven until the final judgment, and of course that they must, in the interval, abide in a separate place. In a note on Hebrews xi. 40, he observes, " The apostle's doctrine, that *believers are " all to be rewarded together, and at the same time*, is " agreeable to Christ's declaration, who told his dis- " ciples that they *were not to come to the place he was " going away to prepare for them, till he returned from " heaven*, to carry them to it." John xiv. 3—" *If I " go and prepare a place for you, I will come again and " receive you unto myself, that where I am, there ye " may be also.*"—Farther, that the *righteous are not to be rewarded till the end of the world*, is evident from Christ's words, Matthew xiii. 40, 43.—In like manner,

St. Peter hath told us, that the righteous are to be *made glad* with their reward, *at the revelation of Christ,* 1 Peter iv. 13, when they are to receive *a crown of glory, that fadeth not away,* 1 Peter v. 4.—John also tells us, that *when he shall appear, we shall be made like him; for we shall see him as he is,* 1 John iii. 2. See Whitby's note on 2 Tim. iv. 8.—This determination, not to reward the ancients without us, is highly proper: because the power and veracity of God will be more illustriously displayed in the view of angels and men, by raising the whole of Abraham's seed from the dead at once, and by introducing them into the heavenly country in a body, after a public acquittal at the judgment, than if *each were made perfect separately at their death.*

If the righteous are not to be rewarded till the end of the world with the glories of heaven, their spirits must remain before that event in some separate place.

Dr. Doddridge, in several passages of his commentary, shows his belief in this doctrine.* He paraphrases the text, (Acts ii. 27,) " Thou wilt not leave my soul " in *Hell*"—thus—" Thou wilt not leave my *soul,* while " *separated* from the body, in the *unseen world.*" And in a note observes, that " ἅδης, (hades) is generally put " for the *state of separate spirits,*" into which he considers that Christ descended.

In a note of Ridgeley's Body of Divinity, the American editor, the Rev. Dr. James P. Wilson, of the Presbyterian Church, states, very correctly, that the Hebrew

---

* Notes on Heb. xi. 40; 2 Tim. iv. 8.

and Greek words translated *Hell* in the passage, " thou
" wilt not leave my soul in Hell," (Psalm xvi. Acts ii.)
" are each taken for the invisible world, or *separate*
" *state of the good as well as evil,* both in the Old and
" New Testaments; and this was thought by Jews
" and Gentiles to be under the surface." Christ's descent into Hell, he observes, therefore, means, that
" his soul, when separated from his body, was imme-
" diately with the *separate spirits who are* happy, and
" so said to be in Paradise. But whether above or
" below the surface, is unimportant."*

It is evident from his commentary on Matthew xi.
23, and on Acts ii. 27, that Dr. Adam Clarke considers that there is a separate place of departed spirits.

There is no doubt that the Rev. John Wesley, the
founder of the sect of which Dr. Clarke is so distinguished a clergyman, maintains this opinion. In his
" Notes upon the New Testament," on Acts ii. 27;
Rev. i. 18; vi. 8; xx. 13, 14, he unequivocally
avows it. On Rev. i. 18—"I have the keys of hell
" and of death," he observes, " that is, the invisible
" world; the body abides in death, and the *soul in*
" *hades*." Rev. xx. 13—" And death and hell gave
" up the dead that were in them," he explains—
" Death gave up all the bodies of men, and *hades*,
" (hell) the *receptacle of separate souls*, gave them up
" to be reunited to their bodies."

Of the *Protestant Episcopal Church*—there is a sermon of the late Bishop Seabury, of Connecticut, on

---

* Ridgeley's Body of Divinity, Am. ed. vol. ii. p. 440, 441, note.

" Christ's descent into Hell," in which the principal
arguments in support of the existence of a separate
place of departed spirits are clearly and concisely exhibited.

In his Lectures on the Catechism, (page 36,) Bishop
White, of Pennsylvania, observes, " It comes in the
" way in this place to notice a very common error
" which has even crept into the public confessions of
" some churches; as if the beatific vision of holy per-
" sons, or their being in Heaven, took place on the dis-
" solution of the body. This is not scriptural. Doubt-
" less such persons are in peace, in *some state answer-*
" *ing to the figurative terms of* ' *Paradise,*' and '*Abra-*
" *ham's bosom;*' with a *measure of bliss,* answering to
" what St. Paul must have implied, when he spoke
" of ' the spirits of just men made perfect.' Still, they
" have not yet reached the state intimated by the same
" apostle, where he speaks of being ' clothed upon
" with our house which is from heaven.' And the sen-
" timent here expressed is sustained by our Church, as
" in many places, so especially when she prays in the
" burial service, for ' perfect consummation and bliss
" both in body and soul.'   But *she no where speaks of*
" *passing immediately from this world to Heaven.*"

Of the *Church of England*—the present Bishop of
Lincoln,* Dr. Tomline, (formerly *Prettyman,)* in his
exposition of the 3d article concerning Christ's descent
into Hell, considers, that by this is meant, " that in the
" intermediate time," between his death and his resur-

* Now Bishop of Winchester, 1824.

rection, " his soul went into the common *receptacle of*
" *departed spirits.*"

Dr. Scott, in his Family Bible, in his commentary on
the 16th Psalm, verse 10, and on Acts ii. 27, speaks
without hesitation of a *separate place of departed spirits* between death and the resurrection.

Dr. Magee,* the celebrated author of " Discourses
" and Dissertations on the Doctrines of Atonement and
" Sacrifice," in a very learned note (page 346, &c.) of
that work, maintains the existence of a *region of departed spirits*—of an *intermediate state of the soul* between its departure from this world and some future
state of its being.

This doctrine is maintained with his usual acumen,
force, and erudition, by Bishop Horsley, in the sermon
quoted in the preceding address, on Christ's Descent
into Hell. In this sermon he maintains the position that
Christ " descended to Hell properly so called, to the
" invisible mansion of departed spirits, and to that
" part of it where the souls of the faithful, after they
" are delivered from the burden of the flesh, are in joy
" and felicity."† In the notes on his commentary on
Hosea, the same doctrine is advanced.

The eloquent and pious Bishop Horne, in his commentary on the 10th verse of the 16th Psalm, maintains the doctrine of the place of departed spirits. " Al-
" though our mortal part must see corruption, yet it
" shall not be finally left under the power of the enemy,
" but shall be raised again and reunited to its old

* Now Archbishop of Dublin, 1824.   † Ser. vol. ii. p. 91.

" companion the *soul, which exists meanwhile in secret*
" *and undiscernable regions, there waiting for the day*
" when its Redeemer shall triumph over corruption in
" his mystical, as he has already done in his natural
" body."

Archbishop Secker, in his Lectures on the Catechism, (Lect. 9,) explaining the descent into Hell, observes—" The most common meaning, not only among
" heathens, but Jews, and the first Christians, of the
" word *Hades*, here translated *Hell*, was in general that
" *invisible world*, one part or another of which, the
" souls of the deceased, whether good or bad, inhabit."
" In what part of space, or of what nature that *recepta-*
" *cle is, in which the souls of men continue from their*
" *death till they rise again*, we scarce know at all; ex-
" cepting, that we are sure it is divided into two ex-
" tremely different regions, the dwelling of the righte-
" ous, called in St. Luke *Abraham's bosom*, where
" *Lazarus* was; and that of the wicked, where the
" *rich man* was; *between which there is a great gulph*
" *fixed*. And we have no proof that our Saviour went
" on any account into the latter; but since he told the
" penitent thief that *he should be that day with him in*
" *paradise*, we are certain he was in the former; where
" *they, which die in the Lord, rest from their labours,*
" and *are* blessed; waiting for a *still more perfect hap-*
" *piness at the resurrection of the last day.*"

The acute and learned " author of the Evidences of
" Natural and Revealed Religion," Dr. Samuel Clarke,
Rector of St. James's, Westminster, in his " Exposi-
" tion of the Church Catechism," explains the word

Hell in the Creed to mean " the invisible state of de-
" parted souls."

Sir Peter King, in his " Critical History of the Apos-
" tles' Creed," proves, at some length, and with great
clearness and force, the existence of a place of departed
spirits, into which Christ descended, in the interval between his death and his resurrection.

Among the sermons of the famous Bishop Bull, the
learned author of the *Defence of the Nicene Faith*, is a
sermon on " the middle state of happiness or misery,"
which he explains and defends in the following terms—
" The *souls* of all the *faithful*, immediately after death,
" enter into a *place and state of bliss*, far exceeding all
" the felicities of this world, though *short of that most*
" *consummate perfect beatitude of the Kingdom of Hea-*
" *ven* with which they are to be crowned and rewarded
" in the resurrection. And so, on the contrary, the
" *souls* of all the *wicked* are, presently after death, in a
" *state of very great misery;* and yet dreading a *far*
" *greater* misery at the day of judgment."* " All *good*
" *men*, without exception, are, in the whole *interval*
" *between their death and resurrection*, as to their souls,
" in a *very happy condition;* but *after* the resurrection
" they shall be *yet more happy*, receiving then their full
" reward, their perfect consummation of bliss, both in
" soul and body, the most perfect bliss they are capa-
" ble of, according to the divers degrees of virtue,
" through the grace of God on their endeavours, at-
" tained by them in this life. On the other side, all

* Bishop Bull's Works, vol. i. p. 102, 103.

" the *wicked, as soon as they die, are very miserable as*
" *to their souls; and shall be yet far more miserable both*
" *in soul and body after the day of judgment,* propor-
" tionably to the measure of sins committed by them
" here on earth.   This is the *plain doctrine* of the *Holy*
" *Scriptures,* and of the *Church of Christ in its first and*
" *best ages,* and this we may trust to."*

Bishop Newton, the author of the " Dissertations on
" the Prophecies," maintains, at considerable length, in
a dissertation in the 6th volume of his works, this doctrine of an intermediate state.

Bishop Pearson, in his " Commentary on the Creed,"
(Art. 5,) observes—" As the sepulchre is appointed for
" our flesh, so there is *another receptacle, or habitation,*
" *or mansion, for our spirits.*   From whence it fol-
" loweth, that in death, the soul doth certainly pass by
" a real motion from that place in which it did inform
" the body, and is translated to *that place,* and unto that
" society, which God, of his mercy or justice, hath
" allotted to it."   " It will appear to have been the
" *general judgment of the Church,* that the *soul of*
" *Christ,* contradistinguished from his body, was truly
" and really carried into *those parts below, where the*
" *souls of men before departed were detained;* and by
" such a real translation of his soul, he was truly
" said to have descended into Hell."   " We must
" confess that the soul of Christ was in Hell, and no
" Christian can deny it," saith St. Augustine.

Bishop Burnet observes, in his " Exposition" of the

3d Article, that " by *Hell* may be meant the *invisible* " place to which departed souls are carried after their " *death*." And, therefore, that by our Saviour's soul descending into Hell, is meant " his soul being removed " out of his body, and carried to those unseen regions " of departed spirits, among whom it continued till his " resurrection."

The pious and learned Bishop Taylor advances the same doctrine in various parts of his writings. In a sermon at the end of his " Worthy Communicant," he observes—" In the *state of separation*, the spirits of " good men shall be blessed and happy souls. They " have an antepast, or taste of their reward ; but their " great reward itself, their crown of righteousness, shall " not be yet. The confirmation of the saint's felicity " shall be at the resurrection of the dead."

Dr. Whitby, in many parts of his " Commentary," and particularly on 2 Tim. iv. 8, advances many arguments from Scripture, to prove that the final and complete happiness of the righteous does not take place until after the judgment at the great day. He considers the immediate ascent of the soul to Heaven, after death, as an heresy contradicted by Scripture, and by the faith of the primitive ages. And he quotes numerous passages from the Fathers to prove that the *souls of good men remain till the day of judgment, in a certain place out of Heaven,* expecting the day of judgment and retribution.

The learned Bingham, in his " Christian Antiqui- " ties," (book xv. chap. 3, sec. 16,) observes, that it was the sense of the primitive Church, that " the *soul*

" is *but in an imperfect state of happiness* till the resur-
" rection, when the *whole man* shall obtain a complete
" *victory over death*, and, by the last judgment, be es-
" tablished in an endless state of consummate happi-
" ness and glory."

The same doctrine of the separate state of departed
spirits is advanced by Wheatley, the author of the
" Commentary on the Book of Common Prayer," and
by Jortin, the author of " Notes on Ecclesiastical His-
" tory," in their *sermons.*

Dr. Nicholls, in his " Commentary on the Book of
" Common Prayer," asserts the same doctrine; interpreting the descent into Hell, of Christ's descent into
the *place of separate souls.*

Dr. Wall, in his " History of Infant Baptism," (part
ii. chap. 8,) goes at considerable length into a statement
of the doctrine of the *intermediate state*, and of the
opinions of the primitive Christians on this point.

Dr. Hammond, in his " Annotations" on 2 Tim.
i. 16, observes—" It is certain that *some measure of*
" *bliss*, which shall, at the day of judgment, be vouch-
" safed the saints, when their bodies and souls shall be
" reunited, is not *till then* enjoyed by them."

There can be no doubt that the *primitive Church*
held this doctrine of the intermediate state.   The opinions of the primitive Fathers are quoted by Bishop
Pearson on the Creed; by Whitby on 2 Tim. iv. 8 ; by
Wall on Infant Baptism, part ii. chap. 8; and by Sir Peter King in his Critical History of the Apostles' Creed.
To their works, and particularly to the latter, the inquisitive reader is referred for information on this point.

III. The doctrine of *a place of departed* spirits, to which the souls of the righteous and the wicked go after death, and where they remain in a state of happiness or misery, expecting their complete felicity or woe in Heaven or Hell, (γίεννα,) after the resurrection at the last day, is a doctrine of *Scripture.*

The leading arguments from Scripture have been already alluded to in the preceding address. It will be proper to recapitulate and amplify them.

In reasoning upon this subject the principle will be assumed, that, with the existence of all created spirits, is essentially connected the idea of *locality. They must exist in some place.* For, as Bishop Horsley observes, (Ser. vol. ii. 89, 90,) " The soul existing after death, " and separated from the body, though of a nature im- " material, must be in some place : for however meta. " physicians may talk of place as one of the adjuncts of " body, as if nothing but gross sensible body could be " limited to a place, to exist with relation to place, " seems to be one of the incommunicable perfections " of the divine Being ; and it is hardly to be conceived, " that any created spirit, of however high an order, can " be without locality, or without such determination of " its existence at any given time to some certain " place, that it shall be true to say of it, ' Here it is, " and not elsewhere.' "

The following view of the state of the departed is also founded on the principle, that *the soul between death and the resurrection, is in a state of consciousness.* The contrary supposition is incompatible with the idea of spirit, of which consciousness seems to be an inseparable attribute. It is opposed by the uniform tenor of Scripture. Abraham, Isaac, and Jacob, all the patriarchs and saints who are departed, are represented as " living unto God." Of course they must be in a state of conscious enjoyment. Moses and Elias appear to our blessed Lord on the mount of transfiguration, and converse with him. The Saviour promised the penitent thief, immediately after death, the reward of bliss with him in Paradise. And the apostle Paul, blessed with the consolations of the divine favour, and with the comforts of the Holy Ghost, looked forward to his state after death, when he should " be with Christ, and be " present with the Lord, as far better."

The apostle was not one of those philosophers who think that the soul cannot exercise its functions, independently of its corporeal companion.

The expression *sleep*, or *sleeping*, so frequently applied in Scripture to the state of the dead, is evidently metaphorical; derived from the resemblance between a *dead* body, and the body of a person *asleep*. The body is said figuratively to " *sleep* in the dust of the " earth;" expecting a resurrection at that day, when the dead, both small and great, shall be summoned to stand before God. Hence the words *cemetery* and *dormitory*, from the Greek and Latin words κοιμάω and *dormio*, to sleep, are applied to the receptacles of the dead.

The comparison between the state of the dead, and a state of sleep, is beautiful and appropriate. Sleep is that relaxation from the toils and afflictions of life, that short suspension of the powers of corporeal sense and action, which are succeeded by a more vigorous exercise of the animal and intellectual faculties. And so death, releasing us entirely from our conflict with the trials of this mortal existence, and suspending all the corporeal functions, is followed by a reviviscence of our whole nature, in the active delights and unalloyed glories of the heavenly state.

The term sleep, applied to the state of the dead, denotes not *unconsciousness*, but a freedom from the cares and labours of life; and, as it respects the righteous, expresses *comfortable enjoyment*, rest, security, and felicity. It is a phrase by which, in all languages, the state of the dead is denoted. And yet the popular belief among all nations, assigned consciousness and activity to the departed.

In שאול the *SHEOL*, or Hell, of the prophets Isaiah and Ezekiel,* the departed monarchs *rise* from their thrones to *meet and to hail* the kings of Babylon and of Egypt.

In the ᾅδης, hades, or *hell*, of Homer, Ulysses, having trod " the downward melancholy way," converses with the shade of his mother, and the " forms of war- " riors slain."† And Virgil represents Æneas, in " faucibus orci,"‡ in the jaws of Hell, in the entrance of Orcus, or the *receptacle of the dead*, as encountering " variarum monstra ferarum," " of various forms un- " numbered spectres." And having passed the bank

---

* Isa. xiv. 9; Ezek. xxxi. xxxii.   † Odyss. xi.
‡ Æneid vi. 273.

5

" irremeabilis undæ," of the " irremeable flood," he holds converse with the shades of the mighty dead.

> —————————— juvat usque morari
> Et conferre gradum et veniendi poscere causas.*
>
> " The gladsome ghosts—
> " Delight to hover near, and long to know
> " What business brought him to the shades below."

The Jews and the heathens had no idea of the state of the departed as a state of insensibility and inaction.

There may be a metaphysical difficulty *how* the soul can exist in an incorporeal state. But does not God, who is a *Spirit*, exert an infinite intelligence and activity, independently of material organs? Did not Jesus, the eternal Word, exist in the spirituality of the Godhead before his incarnation? Does not the Holy Spirit exert his quickening power without the aid of corporeal instruments? Are not angels, those *ministering spirits*, ever occupied in fulfilling the commands of the great Creator—and what is there corporeal in them? When we can account *how* the infinite and eternal persons of the Godhead, and *how* the countless numbers of angelic spirits act independently of body, we may expect to determine in *what mode* the soul acts without the aid of corporeal organs.

But can she not thus act? Undoubtedly. Angelic spirits thus exert intelligence and activity. And the soul thus acts in her present state. Abstraction often renders her forgetful of her corporeal companion, and

---

* Æneid vi. 487.

almost independent of bodily functions. While the body is locked in the benumbing embrace of sleep, the soul wakes, the soul is active, the soul dreams. And may there not be dreams in the sleep of death !

> " To die, to sleep—
> " To sleep! perchance to *dream.*"

The *sleep of the soul* after death, in that sense which supposes it to be *unconscious*, is a modern invention, unknown to the ancient popular creed of both Jews and heathens, repugnant to reason, and contradicted by Scripture.*

With these principles in view, that the *soul exists after death in some place ;* and that she *exists in a state of consciousness;* the following are submitted, as conclusive arguments, from *Scripture*, of the doctrine of the existence of *departed spirits in a separate place, denominated Hades, or Hell, between death and the resurrection.*

I. The Scriptures uniformly represent that there is but *one judgment* at the last day, and that the souls of men are not allotted to Heaven or Hell until this final judgment. Previously to that event, then, the soul must be in some other place. See Matt. xxv. 31, 32; John v. 28, 29, and xii. 48; Acts xvii. 31; Rom. ii. 16; 2 Tim. iv. 1.

II. The happiness of Heaven and the misery of Hell are represented in Scripture as *complete*—the hap-

* In the volumes of the Orthodox Churchman's Magazine, published in England, there are several pieces relative to the intermediate state, and the condition of the soul after death.

piness or misery both of *soul and body.* Matt. xxv.
34, 41; 1 Cor. xv. 52, 53, 54; Phil. iii. 20, 21;
1 Thess. iv. 14, &c.; 2 Thess. i. 7, 8, 9. But until
the resurrection at the last day, the body is subject to
the embrace of corruption. Previously to the resurrection, then, the righteous and the wicked cannot be
in Heaven or Hell. They must be in some other
place. Their state of happiness or misery must be
different from its character in the final Heaven of happiness, and Hell of torment.

III. The apostle asserts, that the saints of the patriarchal and Jewish dispensations have not yet arrived to
the full glory of which they, with the saints of the New
Testament dispensation, will finally partake. Consequently, they cannot be in Heaven, the place of the
final and perfect felicity of the saints. They must be in
some *separate place*, waiting for the perfection of their
bliss. " These," says he, (the saints of old,) " all hav-
" ing obtained a good report by faith, *received not the
promise:* God having provided some better things for
us, that they *without us should not be made perfect.*"*

Doddridge refers this perfection, which the saints
of old do not yet enjoy, but which they will inherit
with us, to the *glory of the heavenly state;* interpreting
the words *they without us, might not be made perfect,*
of God's " purpose of bringing all his children together
" to the *full consummation* of their hopes in Christ
" Jesus his Son, at the time of his final and triumphant
" appearing."†

* Heb. xi. 39, 40.   † Doddridge on Heb. xi. 40.

Whitby, in coincidence with the primitive Fathers, also maintains from this text, that the souls of the Old Testament saints, as well of those who have died under the Christian dispensation, are "*not exalted to the* " *highest heavens;*" that they " had not received their " full reward, yea, that they were not to expect it till " the day of judgment."*

Macknight, in his Commentary on the Epistles, advances the same sentiment, and refers to the arguments of Whitby as sustaining it.†

Wesley, in his notes on this passage observes— " Though they (the Old Testament saints) obtained a " good testimony, yet did not receive the great promise, " the heavenly inheritance—God having provided some " better thing for us, namely, everlasting glory, 'that " they without us should not be made perfect,' that " is, that we might all be perfected together in Hea- " ven."‡

As therefore these saints of old who are *departed* all live to God, for God is " their God," and " God is not " the God of the dead, but of the living;" and as they do not *live* in that state of final glory in heaven, on which they will not enter until the saints under the Gospel are admitted to it, at the judgment of the great day ; it follows, that all departed saints must *live* to God in some *place separate from heaven,* anticipating with *joyful hope* their final glorification.§

* Whitby on Heb. xi. 40.   † Macknight on Heb. xi. 40.
‡ Wesley on Heb. xi. 40.
§ The passage 1 Peter iii. 18, 19, 20, relative to Christ's preaching to the spirits in prison, which was introduced in the preceding

IV. Another argument for the *existence of the departed saints in a separate place*, is founded on the sentiment avowed in Scripture, that *these departed saints have not yet ascended to Heaven.* " No man," says our blessed Lord, " hath ascended up to Heaven, but " he that came down from Heaven, even the Son of " man who is in Heaven."* Enoch and Elijah were translated, according to the foregoing declaration of our Lord, not to that heaven to which Christ hath ascended, and to which he will finally exalt his saints; but to some separate abode of blessedness and peace. It is indeed said, " Elijah went up by a whirlwind into Hea- " ven."† But this mode of expression is agreeable to the popular belief that the state of the blessed is in the

---

address, and more particularly explained in a note, is not here adduced in evidence of the existence of a place of departed spirits, because the interpretation given of this passage rests principally on the authority of a single individual. It seems, however, to the writer, that a serious and deliberate perusal of Bishop Horsley's Sermon on this text will lead, in every case, if not to full conviction, to at least very considerable confidence in the correctness of the interpretation of it, which, with great originality, ingenuity, force, and eloquence, he offers and vindicates.

The learned author of " the Doctrine of the Greek Article," Dr. Middleton (p. 334 of that work) coincides, if not in all the criticisms of Bishop Horsley on this text, at least, in some of the most important. Dr. Middleton, in terms equally just and eloquent, characterizes Bishop Horsley—" To various and recondite " learning, to nervous and manly eloquence, and to powers of rea- " soning, which have been rarely equalled, he added a zeal and in- " trepidity of spirit, which enabled him to prosecute a *glorious*, " though an *unpopular* career, in an heretical and apostate age." Middleton on the Greek Art. p. 334.

* John iii. 13.　　　　† 2 Kings ii. 11.

material heavens. *Heaven* cannot signify that region, wherever it may be in the immeasurable creation of God, which is the scene of the more particular display of the divine glory, to which Christ hath ascended, and to which all his saints are, at the resurrection, to be advanced. This construction of the word would make the passage of the inspired historian directly contradict the assertion of our Lord.

Thus also it is said—" David is not yet ascended " into the Heavens."* His soul, therefore, must abide in some separate region of hope and enjoyment.

The soul then is not in Heaven or in Hell (the *final place of torment)* until after the day of judgment. The happiness or the misery of Heaven and Hell is the happiness or misery of the whole man both body and soul, which are not united until the last day. The saints of old are in joy and felicity, and yet not in *complete* happiness, which they will not receive but in company with all the saints of the Christian dispensation : and these departed saints of old have not yet ascended to Heaven. All these considerations prove that there must be an intermediate state between death and the resurrection, some place distinct from Heaven and Hell (the place of torment) where the souls of the departed abide.

V. This *place of the departed* is particularly designated in Scripture.

It is the ἅδης, *Hades* or *Hell,* into which, agreeably to an article of the Apostles' Creed, our Lord de-

* Acts ii. 34.

scended in the interval between his death and his resurrection.

The existence of a place called Hell, into which Christ descended, is not only asserted in the Apostles' Creed, but in the 3d Article of our Church—" As " Christ died and was buried, so also it is to be believed " that he went down into Hell." Bishop Horsley observes*—" The terms in which the Reformers in this " Article state the proposition, imply that Christ's going " down into Hell is a matter of no less importance to " be believed, than that he died upon the cross for " men; is no less a plain matter of fact in the history " of our Lord's life and death, than the burial of his " dead body."

The doctrine advanced in this Article of the Creed is, that after death, our Lord descended into Hell. This must refer to his *soul*, for his body reposed in the tomb.

As *existence in some place is essential to every created spirit*, the soul of Christ, after death, must have had a particular habitation. This could not be Heaven. There is not the least intimation in Scripture that our Lord ascended there, in the interval between his death and his resurrection. On the contrary, his ascension is always considered as taking place after his resurrection, in his perfect human nature, body as well as soul. In the interval, therefore, between his death and his resurrection, the *soul of our blessed Lord must have abided in some other place than Heaven.*

* Ser. vol. ii. 87.

There are two texts of Scripture which designate the name of this place.

The language of our Lord to the penitent thief—" This day thou shalt be with me in Paradise,"* determines the fact, that the soul of the blessed Jesus after death went to some place, to which, as the habitation of the departed spirits of the *righteous*, the soul of the penitent thief was also admitted; and this place is called *Paradise*. A more particular explanation of this term will be given, when the meaning of the general term " *Hell*," as denoting the place to which our Lord descended, is explained. " Thou wilt not leave my soul " in *Hell;* nor suffer thy Holy One to see corruption."

This passage of the 16th Psalm is expressly applied by St. Peter (Acts ii. 27,) to our Saviour. According to this prediction, the *soul* of Christ was to be in Hell. But he was not in Hell before his death, neither was he there after his resurrection. It follows, that *in the interval between his death and his resurrection, his soul was in Hell.*

There is no escaping from this conclusion, but by maintaining, according to the opinion of some commentators, that the soul here meant, is not his *rational or spiritual soul*, but merely his *animal soul or life;* that soul in the Old Testament means sometimes a dead body; and that therefore the signification of the passage is, *thou wilt not leave my life, my dead body, in the grave;* thou wilt raise me from the dead.

There is no doubt that the words in the original

* Luke xxiii. 43.

6

Hebrew and Greek, which are here translated *soul*, are
used for the animal life, or the dead body of a man.
But they also denote the *rational soul*, the soul properly
so called.

The word translated *soul* in the passage as it occurs
in the 16th Psalm, is in the original נפש, *nephesh*, answering to the Greek ψυχή, (Acts ii. 27.) It occurs,
Deut. vi. 5—"Thou shalt love the Lord thy God
" with all thy heart, and with all thy *soul*" *(nephesh.)*
Here soul is evidently used in the sense of the *rational
soul*, of the *soul or mind*, properly so called; that principle within us which thinks, and understands, and
wills, and exercises the powers, and faculties, and pro-
pensities of our nature. The Hebrew word *nephesh*,
or *soul*, is used in the same signification in other passages of the Old Testament.*

But our principal concern is with the meaning of
the Greek term ψυχή, corresponding to *nephesh*. If
this is used by the writers of the New Testament to
denote the *rational and immortal soul;* as St. Peter
rendered the Hebrew word *(nephesh)* by this term;
it will follow that he understood soul in this passage of
the *rational and immortal soul* of Christ. The following passage establishes the use of the word ψυχή, or
soul, to denote the *rational and immortal part of our
nature:* "Fear not them which kill the body, but are
" not able to kill the soul (ψυχή); but rather fear him
" which is able to destroy both soul (ψυχή) and body
" in hell," (γέεννα, *gehenna*, not ἅδης, Matt. x. 28,) that

* Deut. iv. 29; Psalm xxiv. 4, &c.

is, to punish in the torments of hell the *spiritual and immortal* part of man as well as his corporeal nature. It is applied to the human soul or spirit, as distinguished from his body in other passages of Scripture.*

Since, then, the words translated soul are used in the original to denote the spiritual and immortal part of man, we are justified, unless some sufficient reasons are assigned to the contrary, in thus interpreting them, in the passage which speaks of the *soul* of our blessed Lord not being left in Hell.

---

* Matt. xi. 29; Matt. xxvi. 38 ; John xii. 27. Schleusner observes (Lex. art. ψυχή 6.) that the words translated *heart* and *mind, spirit* and *soul,* are often joined without reference to any subtle distinction in their meaning. Stockius gives *animus,* the *rational and intelligent soul,* as one acceptation of the word ψυχή.

Homer uses ψυχή to denote that *part of man which remains after death.* Thus, in his Odyssey (book xi. 536, 539,) where Ulysses describes his visit to the infernal regions, " ψυχή Αἰακίδαο," anima Æacidæ, or as we would say, the *soul* of Achilles; and " ψυχαὶ νεκρῶν," *animæ mortuorum,* the *souls* of the dead, are the terms by which the dead are distinguished. Virgil uses the term *anima,* corresponding to ψυχή, in the same sense. Thus, (Æn. vi. 264,) " imperium animarum," the empire of *Ghosts,* or, as we would say, of departed *souls.* "Quidve petunt *animæ,*" What do the *Ghosts* desire? or, as we would say, What do the departed *souls* desire?

Ψυχή is applied to the *spiritual and immortal* part of man, by the Greek Fathers. Suicer, in his *Thesaurus,* states that this word is employed by them in its proper signification to denote the *rational soul,* the most *noble and excellent part of man, spiritual and immortal.* He quotes numerous examples of this signification of the word from the Greek Fathers.

There are the most decisive reasons to justify this interpretation. For,

1. If the *soul* in this passage does not mean the *spiritual and immortal part* of man, but is synonymous with *animal life* or dead body, the obvious meaning of the passage, as referring to the two distinct parts of the human nature of Christ, is lost. The last clause of the passage is not a repetition of the former; there is an opposition between them, so far as that they convey distinct meanings, and refer to different things. "Thou " wilt not leave my soul in Hell; neither wilt thou suffer " thy Holy One to see corruption." But if soul refers to the dead body, or to the animal life, the force of the passage is entirely lost. If this were the sense of the words, as Bishop Burnet observes,* " there will be no " opposition in the two parts of this period; the one " will be only a redundant repetition of the other. " Therefore it is much more natural to think, that this " other branch concerning Christ's soul being left in " Hell, *must relate to that which we commonly under-* " *stand by soul.*" If then his " soul was not left in " Hell, from thence it plainly follows, that once it was " in Hell, and by consequence that Christ's soul de- " scended into Hell." Bishop Burnet considers this text as " unquestionable authority that our Saviour's " soul was in Hell."

King, in his " History of the Apostle's Creed," gives the same application to the word soul; observing,

---

* Exposition of the Articles, Art. iii.

" Although the word soul may, by a metonymy, be
" taken in Scripture for the *body*, yet *it cannot be so*
" *understood when it is placed in opposition to and con-*
" *tradistinction from it, as in* this text it is."*

2. According to the interpretation which is here
opposed, there is no account given of the *soul of Christ*,
in the interval between his death and his resurrection—
the whole passage merely affirms the condition of his
body. But if the former clause of the passage be interpreted of the *soul or spiritual part of* the human
nature of Christ, as the latter undoubtedly is of his
body, there is then a full account of the condition of
both parts of his nature. His *soul* was in *Hell*, but not
left there—his *body* in the *grave*, but did not see corruption.

3. It is evident, that some part of the human nature
of the blessed Jesus, called his *soul*, was to be left in
some place called *Hell.* " Thou wilt not leave my
" soul in Hell; neither wilt thou suffer thy Holy One
" to see corruption." His *body* was to be in the grave,
but was not to see corruption, his *soul* was not to be
left in Hell. But if *soul* means merely his animal life,
this not being a distinct subsistence, there was no part of
his nature in Hell. Soul must therefore refer to some
distinct part of the human nature of our blessed Lord,
which was not left in Hell. The term soul ($\psi v \chi \eta$) cannot mean his body ; it cannot mean his *animal life,*
which was no *distinct subsistence:* it must mean his
soul properly so called, the spiritual and immortal part

* History of the Apostle's Creed, Art. Descent into Hell.

of his human nature. This, his *soul, properly so called,* was in Hell, but was not left there.

4. This passage was understood of the descent of the *rational and intellectual soul of Christ* into Hell, by the primitive Church. Bishop Pearson, in his learned work on the Creed, observes,* that it was " the general " judgment of the Church, that the *soul* of Christ con- " tradistinguished from his body, that better and more " noble part of his humanity, his *rational and intellectual* " *soul,* after a true and proper separation from his flesh, " was really and truly carried into those parts below, " where the souls of men before departed were de- " tained; and by such a real translation of his soul, " he was truly said to have descended into Hell." There is *nothing in which the Fathers more agreed* than this, a *real descent of the soul of Christ unto the habitation of the souls departed.* The persons to whom, and end for which, he descended, they differ in; but as to a *local descent into the infernal parts, they all agree.* Referring to the passage under consideration, " Thou wilt not leave my soul in Hell," Bishop Pearson does not hesitate to observe, " From this place, the " article (of the descent into Hell) is *clearly and infalli-* " *bly* deduced thus: If the soul of Christ were not left " in Hell at his resurrection, then his *soul was in Hell* " before his resurrection. But it was not there before " his death; therefore, upon or after his death, and " before his resurrection, *the soul of Christ descended* " *into Hell;* consequently the Creed doth *truly deliver*

* On the Creed, Art. Descent into Hell.

" that Christ being *crucified*, was *dead*, *buried*, and
" *descended into Hell.* For as his *flesh did not see*
" *corruption* by virtue of that promise and prophetical
" expression, and yet it was *in the grave*, the place of
" corruption, where it rested in hope until his resurrec-
" tion; so his *soul*, which was *not left in Hell*, by
" virtue of the like promise or prediction, was in that
" Hell, where it was not left, until the time that it was
" to be united to the body for the performing of the
" resurrection. *We must therefore confess from hence,*
" *that the soul of Christ was in Hell; and no Christian*
" *can deny it, saith St. Augustine, it is so clearly de-*
" *livered in this prophecy of the Psalmist, and applica-*
" *tion of the Apostle.*"*

---

* Bishop Pearson on the Creed, Art. *He descended into Hell*,
Oxford edit. 1797, p. 358—360. This Article, He descended into
Hell, was not introduced into the Creed, until about three hundred
years after Christ. But it will not follow that Christ's descent
into Hell was not previously a doctrine of the Church. On the
contrary, the Fathers, from the early ages, maintained this opinion,
as Bishop Pearson observes, who quotes at length their opinions.
The clause was first introduced into the Creed of the Church of
Aquiliea, in which there was no mention of Christ's burial. It
would not hence follow, that these words referred *solely* to the
burial of Christ's body : since his " descent into Hell," neces-
sarily denoting the descent of his body into the grave, *might* also
imply the descent of his soul into Hades or Hell. As Bishop
Pearson observes, " Although they were first put into the Aquiliean
" Creed, to signify the burial of Christ, and those which had only
" the burial in their Creed, did confess as much as those which
" without the burial did express the descent; yet since the Roman
" Creed hath added the descent unto the burial, and expressed that
" descent by words signifying more properly *Hell*, it cannot be
" imagined that the Creed, as it now stands, should signify only

Sir Peter King* gives the same view of the opinion
of the Primitive Fathers—" They apply this action of
" our Saviour's to his soul alone, employing for this
" end that text of the Apostle cited by him from the
" Psalmist, on which this Article is principally founded
" (Acts ii. 27.) By the soul of Christ, which God
" would not leave in Hell, they understood the *rational*
" *part* of man, that *spirit* which distinguishes him from
" a brute, and subsists after its disunion and departure
" from the body."

5. It may be observed—That by denying, that the
descent of Christ into Hell in this passage, is meant of
the descent of his *soul properly so called*, we give up
the principal argument from Scripture, of the *existence
of the human soul of Christ*. Apollinaris, an early
heretic, denied to Christ an *intellectual or rational soul*,
the place of which was supplied, he said, by the *Word*,
or Divinity. Against this heresy, the orthodox urged
the text relative to Christ, " Thou wilt not leave my
" soul in Hell." Christ's descent into Hell, they considered as an undeniable proof that he had a *reasonable
soul*. For it could not be his *deity* that descended into
Hell; that being omnipresent, was incapable of any

" the burial of Christ by his descent into Hell." " The ancient
" Church did certainly believe that Christ did some other way
" descend beside his burial; Ruffinus himself, (an ecclesiastical
" writer) though he interpreted those words of the burial only,
" yet in the relation of what was done at our Saviour's death,
" makes mention of his *descent into Hell beside, and distinct from*
" his sepulture; and those, who in after ages added it to the
" burial, did actually believe that the soul of Christ descended."

* History of the Apostle's Creed, Descent into Hell.

local transition. It could not be his *body;* for that was committed to the tomb. It must have been his *reasonable, human soul,* which descended there, since there is no evidence of the existence, after death, of the *animal,* or sensitive part of our nature, which we have in common with the brutes. To maintain, then, that the text— " Thou wilt not leave my *soul* in Hell," is meant of the sensitive nature, the animal life of Christ, subverts entirely the principal argument in favour of the reality of his *reasonable soul,* which the Catholic or universal Church urged against the Apollinarian heresy. As Bishop Pearson, in his reasoning on this subject, observes, —" If it could have been answered by the heretics, as " it is now by many, that his descent into Hell had no " relation to his *soul,* but to his *body only, which de-* " *scended into the grave;* or that it was not a real, but " virtual descent, by which his death extended to the " destruction of the powers of Hell; or that his soul " was not his *intellectual spirit,* or immortal soul, but " his *living soul,* which descended into Hell; that is, " continued in the state of death; I say, if any of these " senses could have been affixed to this Article, (the " descent into Hell,) the Apollinarian's answer might " have been sound, and the Catholic's argument of no " validity. But since those heretics did all acknow- " ledge this Article; since the Catholic Fathers did " urge the same to prove the *real distinction* of the " *soul* of Christ, both from his *divinity,* and from his " *body,* because his body was really in the grave, when " his soul was really present with the souls below; it " followeth that it was the general doctrine of the

7

" Church, that Christ did descend into Hell, by a local
" motion of his soul separated from his body to the
" places below, where the souls of men departed were."

" Nor can it be reasonably objected that the argu-
" ment of the Fathers was of equal force against these
" heretics, if it be understood of the *animal soul*, as it
" would be if it were understood of the *rational;* as if
" those heretics had equally deprived Christ of the ra-
" tional and animal soul. For it is most certain that
" they did not deprive Christ of both; but most of the
" Apollinarians denied an human soul to Christ only
" in respect to the *intellectual* part, granting that the
" animal soul of Christ was of the same nature with
" the animal soul of other men. If, therefore, the Fa-
" thers had proved only that the *animal soul* of Christ
" had descended into *Hell*, they had brought no argu-
" ment at all to prove that Christ had an *human intel-*
" *lectual soul*. It is, therefore, certain, that the Catholic
" Fathers, in their opposition to the Apollinarian here-
" tics, did declare, that the *intellectual and immortal*
" *soul of Christ descended into Hell*."*

If we deny the descent of the *soul* of Christ, properly so called, into *Hell*, we relinquish the principal
argument in favour of the *doctrine* of the *real incarnation* of Christ, against the heretics which have assailed
it. The Apollinarians and Nestorians denied to Christ
a *rational soul.* They maintained that the two natures
in Christ, the *divine* and the *human*, were not united,
but that God dwelt in Christ as his temple, supplying

* Pearson on the Creed, vol. i. p. 359, 360. Oxford edit. 1797.

the place of the rational soul. And the Eutychians, on the contrary, asserted the *confusion of natures* in Christ; so that there was in him but one nature—the *divine*. In opposition to these heresies, the true doctrine of the incarnation is, that Jesus Christ is " per- " fect God and perfect man ; of a reasonable soul and " human flesh subsisting ; and as the *reasonable soul* " and flesh is one man, so God and man is one Christ."

Bishop Pearson observes*—" The true doctrine of " the incarnation, against all the enemies thereof, Apol- " linarians, Nestorians, Eutychians, and the like, was " generally expressed by declaring the verity of the " *soul of Christ really present in Hell,* and the verity " of his body at the same time really present in the " grave."

It appears, then, that by considering the passage— " Thou wilt not leave my soul in Hell," as indicating, not the *intellectual soul,* but *the animal soul or life ;* and not *the place of departed spirits,* but merely the *grave ;* we shall vary from the belief of the universal Church in the earlier ages, and relinquish the principal argument against many of the most dangerous here- sies relative to the person and nature of our blessed Lord.

It was necessary to go into this view of the subject, because it is maintained by many useful and able com- mentators and critics, that this passage merely denotes, *thou wilt not leave my life in the grave.* Dr. Whitby,

---

* Vol. ii. p. 306.

at considerable length, maintains this opinion, which is also held by the learned Parkhurst, and others.   It ought to be observed, however, that Whitby and Parkhurst are strong advocates for an *intermediate state ;* and the former admits that the soul of Christ was in Paradise after his death.   " The Scripture doth assure " us, that the soul of the Holy Jesus, being separated " from his body, went to Paradise."* (Luke xxiii. 43.)

The opposite construction of this passage, as applicable to the descent of the *rational soul* of Christ to Hell, is supported by the opinion of the primitive Fathers and Commentators; and of *modern Critics and Expositors* of great name, among whom rank, Bishop Pearson, Bishop Horsley, Dr. Campbell, Dr. Doddridge, and Dr. Adam Clarke.†

Bishop Pearson's views of this passage have been already fully stated.

Bishop Horsley observes‡—that " these words of the " Creed, ' he descended into Hell,' declare what was " done by his *rational soul* in its intermediate state." And afterwards, quoting the passage which has been under discussion, " Thou wilt not leave my soul," &c. proceeds thus—" *From this text, if there were no*

---

* Whitby's Com. vol. ii. p. 267.

† None of these authors, however, present a *full and particular* answer to the formidable argument, urged with great force by respectable Commentators and Critics, that *soul* in this passage means the *animal life.* Bishop *Horsley* takes no notice of it. Dr *Campbell* merely adverts to it.   Bishop *Pearson* answers it somewhat in detail.   *King* incidently notices it in his History of the Apostles' Creed.

‡ Scr. vol. ii. p. 88.

" other, *the Article, in the sense in which we have ex-*
" *plained it, is clearly and infallibly deduced;* for if the
" soul of Christ were not left in Hell *at* his resurrec-
" tion, then it *was* in Hell *before* his resurrection. But
" it was not there either before his death or after his
" resurrection, for that never was imagined : therefore
" it descended into Hell after his death, and before his
" resurrection ; for as his flesh, by virtue of the divine
" promise, saw no corruption, although it was in the
" grave, the place of corruption, where it remained
" until his resurrection ; so his soul, which, by virtue
" of the like promise, was not left in Hell, was *in* that
" Hell where it was not *left,* until the time came for its
" reunion to the body for the accomplishment of the
" resurrection. Hence it is so clearly evinced, that the
" soul of Christ was in the place called Hell, ' that
" none but an infidel,' saith St. Augustine, ' can deny
" it.' "

Dr. Campbell vindicates the same construction of
this passage.

Dr. Doddridge paraphrases the words—" Thou wilt
" not leave my soul in Hell"—thus—" I am fully satis-
" fied, that thou wilt not leave my *soul while separated*
" *from it (the body)* in the *unseen world.*" And, in
opposition to the opinion advanced by Whitby, and
others, that the soul here is put for the *animal life or
dead body,* and ἅδης, Hades, for the grave, he observes,
in a note—" As ψυχή, which is the word here used,
" can hardly be thought to signify a dead body, and
" ἅδης is generally put for the state of separate spirits,

" the version here given seemed preferable to any
" other."

Dr. Adam Clarke interprets the same words of the
soul of Christ not being left in *the state of separate
spirits.*

The opposite construction which has been given of
this passage, and the hostility to the doctrine of an intermediate state, and of the descent of Christ into Hell,
among many Protestant divines, appear to have arisen
from an apprehension of countenancing the papal doctrine of purgatory, to which, however, the primitive and
correct doctrine of the state of separate spirits gives no
countenance.

But it is of primary importance, in this discussion,
to ascertain the correct meaning of the word which, in
this passage, and many others of the sacred writings, is
translated *Hell.* If this mean a *place of departed spirits,* then of course the existence of this place is not
only established, but also the *descent of* the *spirit or
soul* of Christ into the same abode.

The word *Hell,* in our English translation of the
Bible, answers in the original to two distinct words,
ᾅδης, (Hebrew, *Sheol,)* Hades, denoting merely a secret, invisible place, and hence applied to the *place of
departed spirits;* and γέεννα, Gehenna, signifying the
place of final torment.

There can be no doubt that the acceptance of the
word αἴδης, or ᾅδης, Hades, among the Greeks, was the
place of the departed. In the commencement of the

Iliad, it was to " αἴδι." " Pluto's gloomy reign," that the anger of Achilles hurled

> " The souls of mighty chiefs untimely slain."

Answering to the ἄδης of the Greeks, is the *Orcus* of the Romans.   It was the boast of Virgil's heroes.*

> "   ——Multos Danaûm dimittimus Orco."
> " With gods averse we follow to the fight,
> " And undistinguished in the shades of night,
> " Mix with the foes, employ the murdering steel,
> " And *plunge whole squadrons to the depths of Hell.*"

The existence of a region where the departed shades resided, was the popular belief of the Greeks and Romans, and was denoted by the ἀΐδης, or ἄδης, of the one, and the *Orcus*, or *inferi*, of the other.   And it is reasonable to conclude, that the Apostles would use the word ἄδης, Hades, in its popular signification, as denoting the *place of the departed.*

But, to denote the place of final torment, they employed another, γέεννα, Gehenna, a compound of two Hebrew words, signifying the valley of Hinnom.   It was originally a pleasant valley, planted with trees, and watered with fountains, near to Jerusalem, by the brook of Kedron.   The Jews placed there the image of Moloch, to which they sacrificed their children.   When these horrid sacrifices were abolished by *Josiah*, the pious king of Israel, the place became so abominable,

* Æneid ii. 398.

that they cast there the carcases of animals, and the
dead bodies of criminals, where they were consumed
by fire. Hence it was used, to denote the place of future
torment, not only by the Jews, but by Christ and his
Apostles. *Tophet*, from Toph, which signifies a drum,
was a name also applied to this place; the noise of
drums being employed at the sacrifices, to drown the
cries of the victims. And hence *Tophet* also, among
the Jews, denoted the place of future punishment.*

These two words, ἅδης and γέεννα, *Hades* and *Gehenna*, are indiscriminately rendered *Hell* in the New
Testament. But wherever the former word *Hades* is
translated Hell, the *place of departed spirits* is meant;
and wherever *Gehenna* is rendered Hell, the *place of
the damned* is denoted.

The idea of the place of torment is now commonly
connected with this word *Hell*. But the original meaning of the word " Hell" was no more than a *hidden* or
invisible place, from the Saxon word " helan," to cover
over. In this acceptation it is used as the translation of
the Greek word ἅδης, Hades. Dr. Doddridge observes
—(Com. on Rev. i. 18,)—" Our English, or rather
" Saxon word *Hell*, in its original signification (though
" it is now understood in a more limited sense,) exactly
" answers to the Greek word *Hades*, and denotes a
" *concealed* or *unseen* place, and this sense of the word
" is still retained in the eastern, and especially the west-
" ern counties of England; to *hell* over a thing, is to

---

* See *Schleusner's* Lexicon, Art. Γέεννα, and *Campbell's* Prelim.
Dissert. Part ii. 1, and *Calmet's* Dict. Art. Gehenna and Tophet.

" cover it." Dr. Campbell observes—(Prelim. Dissertations, vi. part ii. 2,)—" The term ἅδης, Hades, was " written anciently ἀΐδης, ab a priv. et εἴδω video, and " signifies *obscure, hidden, invisible.* To this the word " *Hell,* in its primitive signification, perfectly corres- " ponded. For at first it denoted only what was *secret* " or *concealed.* This word is found with little varia- " tion of form, and precisely in the same meaning, in " all the Teutonic dialects." " The term *Hades* im- " plies, properly, neither Hell nor the grave, but the " *place or state of departed souls.*"

" The word *Hell,* (says Dr. Adam Clarke,*) used " in the common translation, conveys *now* an improper " meaning of the original word ; because Hell is only " used to signify the place of the damned. But as the " word *Hell* comes from the Anglo-Saxon *helan,* to " cover or hide, hence the tyling or slating of a house " is called, in some parts of England, (particularly " Cornwall,) *heling* to this day, and the covers of books " (in Lancaster) by the same name; so the literal im- " port of the original word Ἅδης was formerly well ex- " pressed by it."†

" The word *Hell,* in its natural import," (says Bi-

* Com. on Matt. xi. 23.

† Dr. Johnson, in his Dictionary, gives, as one meaning of *Hell,* " the place of departed spirits, whether good or bad." But Mr. Webster omits this acceptation of the word, which is founded on its *Saxon derivation;* though he professes that his acquaintance with the Saxon language, " the mother tongue of the English," qualifies him eminently for accurately defining English words.

shop Horsley,*) " signifies only that invisible place
" which is the appointed habitation of departed souls
" in the interval between death and the general resur-
" rection."

In this acceptation of the word *Hell*, as *the place of
the departed*, answering to the ᾅδης of the Greeks,
and the *Orcus* of the Romans, was the term שׁאוֹל,
SHEOL, used among the Jews. It is derived from
שׁאַל, which signifies to *ask*, to *crave*, to *crave as a
loan*.

In the first signification of its derivative, simply to
ask; SHEOL denotes a place which is an object of
universal inquiry, the *unknown* mansion about which all
are anxiously *inquisitive*.

In the second acceptation of its derivative, *SHEOL*
is represented as a place of *insatiable craving;* which
characteristic is frequently assigned it in several parts
of Scripture. " Hell *(Sheol)* hath enlarged herself, and
" opened her mouth without measure," saith the Prophet, (Isa. v. 14.)   " The proud man," (saith another
Prophet, Habakkuk ii. 5,) " enlargeth his desire as
" Hell," (Sheol.)

In the third meaning of the derivative of *Sheol*, to
demand or crave as a loan, implying that what is sought
for is to be *rendered back ;* " SHEOL is to be under-
" stood, not simply as the region of departed spirits,
" but as the region which is to form their *temporary*
" residence, and from which at some future time they
" are to be rendered up; thus indicating an inter-

" mediate state of the soul between its departure
" from this world, and some future state of its exist·
" ence."*

As the *region of the dead*, or *place of the departed*,
Sheol, or Hell, is used in the Old Testament. But the
Hebrew word for the *grave* is קֶבֶר, *Keber*, the receptacle of the dead body, but not of the soul; and accord-
ingly, the Hebrew word for soul, *Nephesh*, is never
joined with *Keber*, but with *Sheol*, the term denoting
the abode of departed spirits.† The Hebrew *Sheol* is
never used for the grave, though it is sometimes translated by this word. This, Bishop Horsley proves with
his usual acumen—" Although Keber (the grave) is
" never used for *Sheol*, to signify Hell ; there are five
" texts in which the contrary may seem to have taken
" place; namely, the use of *Sheol* for *Keber*, to signify
" the repository of the body, rather than the mansion of
" the departed spirit.   These five texts are—Gen.
" xlii. 38 ; xliv. 29 and 31 ; 1 Kings ii. 6 and 9. But,
" upon consideration, it will appear, that in every one
" of these, the thing to be expressed is neither ' Hell,'
" nor ' the grave,' particularly, and as distinct the one
" from the other ; but the state of death : and this state
" is expressed under the image of a place of residence
" of the dead collectively.   And for this place, taken
" in the gross, not as divided into the two separate
" lodgments of the spirit and the carcase, the word

---

* See Magee on the Atonement, &c. p. 348, note; and Horsley's Com. on Hosea, p. 158.

† Peters on Job, p. 320.

" שְׁאוֹל is used.   It is, therefore, very ill rendered by
" the word 'grave,' even in these texts; and ' Hell'
" would be a better rendering; because the only ge-
" neral place of residence of the dead collectively is
" that of the departed spirit.   The grave is no general
" place, since every dead body has its own appropriate
" grave.   Perhaps, in these instances, the word *Sheol*
" would be best expressed, in English, by a periphra-
" sis, 'region of the dead,' or 'dwelling of the dead,'
" or ' the nether regions.' "

There is yet a sixth text, Psalm cxli. 7, in which we
read, in the English Bible, of " bones scattered at the
" grave's mouth ;" but, in the Hebrew—" at the mouth
" of *Sheol*."   This passage is often alleged, as an evident instance of the use of שְׁאוֹל for the grave.   But
the fact is, that here we have no mention of the grave
at all.   For the Psalmist is clearly speaking of the
bones of persons massacred, whose bodies never were
in any grave, but had been left to rot, unburied, upon
the surface of the earth.   And the mouth of *Sheol* in
this surface, considered as the entrance of *Sheol;*
which, in the imagery of the sacred writers, as well as
of the oldest Greek poets, is always considered as in
the central parts of the earth's hollow sphere.*

The word *SHEOL*, and in the Septuagint, Hades,
first occurs in Gen. xxxvii. 34, and is translated *grave*.
Jacob says—" I will go down into the *grave* to my
" son, mourning."   But the rendering should be—" I
" will go down to Hades, to *Hell*," that is, to the place

---

* Com. on Hosea, p. 200.

of the departed, " to my son, mourning." The patriarch did not mean that he should go into the grave to
his son, for then *KEBER*, which literally signifies the
grave, as it is, Gen. xxxv. 20, " and Jacob set a pillar
" upon Rachel's grave," would have been used. His
son also he supposed was torn in pieces by a wild beast,
and, therefore, the idea of his literally going down to
him in the *grave* would not have naturally occurred.
But if we consider the word *Sheol* as denoting the
place of the departed, we give a forcible and natural
meaning to the declaration of the patriarch.

Bishop Patrick observes, on this passage, that
" *SHEOL* must signify the *state or place of the dead*,*
" as it often doth."† Lowth remarks‡—" The word
" *Sheol* cannot be understood of the grave properly so
" called, because Jacob thought his son was devoured
" by some wild beast; but must be meant of *the*
" *place* where he supposed Joseph's soul was lodged."
Archbishop Secker asserts—" The translation *into the*
" *grave* is wrong; as if he meant to have his body laid
" by Joseph's. That could not be, for he thought him
" devoured by wild beasts. It means into the *invisi-*
" *ble state*, the state of departed souls; and in this
" sense, it is said of several of the patriarchs, that they
" ' were gathered unto their people,' Gen. xxv. 8;
" Gen. xxxv. 29; and of ' all that generation' which

---

* "Region of the dead." is synonymous with the *place of the
departed*, because, as Bishop Horsley observes, (Com. on Hosea,
p. 200)—" The only general place of residence of the dead col-
" lectively, is that of the departed spirit."

† Patrick on Gen. xxxv. ‡ Lowth on Isa. xiv. 9.

" lived with Joshua, that they ' were gathered unto
" their fathers.' "

The learned Vitringa, in his Commentary on Isaiah,*
quotes this passage, and several others in the Old Testament, in which he says the word *Sheol* ought to be
translated not *grave*, but *Hell*, in the sense of a receptacle of departed spirits.

It is almost needless to remark, that the word
SHEOL, or Hades, in this passage, could not possibly
mean the state of the damned.

In the book of Job,† there is a very sublime description of the power of the Almighty. " *Hell* is
" naked before him." The word " Hell," in the original, is *Sheol*, and means the *state or place of the departed*. So it is understood by the learned Commentators on Job, Schultens and Peters ; by Patrick, by
Lowth, and by Scott, the latter of whom thus paraphrases it—" Neither the *bodies* which, all over the
" earth, are laid in the *grave*, nor the *state of the de-
" parted souls of men*, are concealed from his all-seeing
" eye."

Dr. Magee, in a Dissertation on the History and
Book of Job, annexed to his *Discourses on the Atonement*, gives a new rendering of the passage which contains the above verse. He founds it on the opinion of
the Jews, who held " Gehenna, or the place of perdi-
" tion, to be the lowest part of Sheol, the general recep-
" tacle of departed souls : and that, in order to express
" the great depth to which they conceive it to be sunk,

* Com. on Isa. xiv. 9, p. 433.   † Job xxvi. 6.

" they are used to describe it as *beneath the waters :*
" their idea being, that the waters are placed below the
" earth. *Tartarus*, in like manner, the Greeks made
" the lowest part of Hades, (Windet de vita functorum
" statu."*)

On this Jewish notion of Sheol, or *Hell*, Dr. Magee gives a new rendering to the two verses of Job
xxvi. 5, 6, which stand in our translation thus :—

> 5 Dead things are formed
> From under the waters and the inhabitants thereof.

> 6 *Hell* is naked before him,
> And destruction hath no covering,-

Dr. Magee renders them thus:—

> 5 " The souls of the dead tremble ;
> " [The places] below the waters, and their inhabitants.

> 6 " The seat of spirits is naked before him :
> " And the region of destruction hath no covering."

" Here I take the *souls of the dead*, and the *inhabitants*
" *of the places below the (abyss of) waters*, to bear to

---

* Magee's Dissertations on the Atonement, &c. p. 349. In a
note to Lowth's Lectures on Hebrew Poetry, (vol. i. p. 213,) it is
observed—" That the place where the wicked, after death, were
" supposed to be confined, was believed, from the destruction of
" the old world by the *deluge*, the covering of the Asphaltic vale
" with the *Dead Sea*, &c. to be situated *under the waters*. To this
" idea," which certainly very naturally accounts for the popular
belief on this subject, " there are allusions in the sacred writings
" without number."

" each other the same proportion, that is found in the
" next verse to subsist between the *seat of spirits*, and
" the *region of destruction :* those of the dead who
" were sunk in the *lowest parts* of Sheol, being placed
" in the *region of destruction*, or the *Gehenna* of the
" later Jews.   So that the passage, on the whole, con-
" veys this—that nothing is, or can be, concealed from
" the all-seeing eye of God ; that the souls of the dead
" tremble under his view, and the shades of the wicked
" sunk to the bottom of the abyss, can even there find
" no covering from his sight."

In the sublime passage of the Prophet *Isaiah*, (chap.
xiv.) where the deceased tyrants are represented as
rising to meet the king of Babylon, and in the passages
of the Prophet Ezekiel, (xxxi. xxxii.) where the same
description is applied to the king of Egypt, Hell,
without doubt, signifies the *place of the departed.*   In
the Prophet Ezekiel, " the strong among the mighty,"
are represented as speaking to him, the king of Egypt,
" out of the midst of Hell."   The elder Lowth, in his
Commentary, considers the whole passage as " a poeti-
" cal description of the *infernal regions*, where the
" ghosts of deceased tyrants, with their subjects, are
" represented as coming to meet the king of Egypt,
" and his auxiliaries, upon their arrival to the same
" place : *Hell* signifies here the *state of the dead.*"   On
the passage in Isaiah xiv. 9—" Hell from beneath is
" moved for thee," Lowth remarks—" the Hebrew
" word *Sheol*, which our translation renders *Hell*, or
" the *grave*, signifies the *state of the dead* in general,
" and is indifferently applied to the *good and bad.*"

" Thus then," as Dr. Magee observes, " in like manner
" as *Homer*, in his *Odyssey*, sends the souls of the
" slaughtered wooers to *Hades*, where they meet with
" the manes of Achilles, Agamemnon, and other he-
" roes; so the Hebrew poet, in this passage of inimit-
" able grandeur, describes the king of Babylon, when
" slain and brought to the grave, as entering *Sheol*,
" and there meeting the *Rephaim*, or manes of the
" dead, who had descended thither before him, and
" who are poetically represented as rising from their
" seats at his approach.   And as, on the one hand, the
" passage in the Grecian bard has been always held,
" without any question, to be demonstrative of the
" existence of a popular belief amongst the Greeks,
" that there was a place called *Hades*, which was the
" receptacle for departed souls: so this poetic image of
" Isaiah must be allowed, upon the other, to indicate, in
" like manner, amongst the Jews, the existence of a
" popular belief that there was a region for departed
" souls called *Sheol*, in which the *Rephaim* or manes
" took up their abode."

Bishop Lowth, in his lectures and commentary,
considers this passage as a personification of the *grave*.
But the learned Vitringa proves that it is a representation, not of the *grave*, but of *Hell*, the receptacle of
departed souls.

In his Commentary on Isaiah,* he states that it was
the common opinion among the Jews, and the Greeks,
and the Romans, that there was a receptacle of separate

* Vitringa's Com. Isa. chap. xiv. part i. p. 432, 433.

spirits, to which the Jews gave the name שְׁאוֹל, *Sheol*,
the Greeks ᾄδης, and the Latins *Inferi*, all answering to
the English word *Hell*.   He quotes several examples
from the Old Testament to prove that the Jews considered *Hell* as the receptacle of separate spirits, who,
they thought, were not deprived of consciousness after
death.   And this opinion, he states expressly, was not
erroneous.

There are some learned men who incline to the
opinion, that the Jews derived their notions of a future
state from the Pagan writers.   But the contrary opinion
is much more probable, that the Pagan views of the
state of the dead were corruptions of the early patriarchal revelations.   As the learned Calmet observes,*
" The Hebrews thought and spoke almost like the
" Greeks before Homer, Hesiod, and the most ancient
" poets of this nation."   Moses speaks of " the lowest
" Hell."†   Job, " Hell is naked before God."‡   Solo-
mon, " Hell and destruction are before the Lord."§
Here Hell, as the place of the departed, is spoken of by
Jewish writers who preceded the most ancient Greek
poets.   In the opinion that the Pagans derived their
views of the state of the dead from the ancient Hebrews, Calmet is supported by Bishop Horsley, and
by the learned Vitringa.‖

---

* Calmet's Dic. Art. Hell.   The English edition of Calmet, by
D'Oyly and *Calson*, is here quoted.   The modern edition by *Taylor*,
has very seriously mutilated the original work ; though the " Frag-
" ments" that are annexed, are many of them valuable additions.
   † Deut. xxxii. 22.   ‡ Job xxvi. 5.   § Prov. xv. 11.
‖ Com. on Isa. xiv. 9.

The opinions of the ancient Hebrews, and of the Heathen at large, concerning the place of the departed, are represented at length by Vitringa. A compressed statement of his detail of their opinions is given by Archbishop Magee,* " That the souls of men, when " released from the body by death, pass into a vast sub- " terraneous region, as a common receptacle, but with " different mansions, adapted to the different qualities of " its inhabitants: and that here, preserving the shades " and resemblances of the living, they fill the same cha- " racters they did in life.—That this entire region was " called by the Jews *Sheol*, by the Greeks *Hades*, and " by the Latins *Inferi*.—That these were the notions " that commonly prevailed amongst the Jews, he con- " ceives to be fully established by various parts of " Scripture: and to this, he thinks, the history of the " witch of Endor yields confirmation, inasmuch as, let " the illusion in that transaction be what it might, it " goes to establish the fact of the opinion which was " then vulgarly received.—Agreeably to this hypothesis, " he contends, that various expressions of the patri- " archs and prophets are to be explained; and to this " purpose he instances Gen. xxxvii. 35; Ps. xvi. 10; " xxx. 3; xciv. 17; in all of which, a place where souls, " when freed from the body, were assembled, still " preserving all their faculties,—is, as he thinks, plainly " supposed.—From the Hebrews, he conceives that " this opinion passed to the other people, and became " disfigured by various fictions of their respective in-

* Magee on the Atonement, p. 346, &c.

" vention. Thus the doctrine of the Egyptians re-
" specting *Hades*, is given in the second book of
" Herodotus; where we have the history of Rhamp-
" sinitus, who, according to the traditions of the Egyp-
" tians, had visited the infernal regions and returned
" safe to life. The notion, he says, was variously
" embellished by the Greek poets: and afterwards,
" being stripped by Plato of much of its poetic orna-
" ments, was embodied by him in his philosophical
" system. Hence again the Latins and the nations at
" large, derived their phraseology in speaking of the
" state of the dead; for instances of which phraseology
" he refers to *Velleius*, *Livy*, *Florus*, and others."

The Greeks and Romans then, had their *place of the
departed*, to which they gave the names of ᾅδης and
orcus. The Hebrews had their *place of the departed*,
which they denominated שְׁאוֹל SHEOL; and which
the Septuagint, in the sense of the Greek ᾅδης, *Hades*,
translated by this term. The place of the departed,
Bishop Horsley observes, is the only " Hell of the Old
" Testament."*

It cannot be supposed that the writers of the New
Testament were strangers to the popular belief of their
countrymen, and of the Heathen generally, with respect
to the region of the departed. When they used the
term ᾅδης, Hades, they undoubtedly used it in its
settled, universal, and appropriate signification of the
place of departed spirits. This was the signification
which the authors of the *Septuagint* translation of the

* Bishop Horsley's Com. on Hosea, p. 46.

Old Testament annexed to the term. Except in a very few instances, they have translated the Hebrew word *Sheol*, which occurs in above sixty places in the Old Testament, not by θάνατος, death, by τάφος, the grave, by μνῆμα or μνημεῖον, the sepulchre; but by ἅδης, Hades, the appropriate word for the *region of the dead*, for the *place of the departed*, in a state of consciousness. The writers of the New Testament quote from this Septuagint translation, in which the word *Hades* is put for *Sheol*. They must therefore have considered *Hades* as expressing, what *Sheol* does in the Old Testament, the *place of departed souls*.

The inquiry as to the *situation* of this place of departed spirits, cannot be important. It is sufficient to know that there is a place of residence assigned them, in some part of the vast universe of God.

Bishop Horsley, with great ingenuity, advocates the opinion that the receptacle of the departed is in the inner parts of the earth. " It is evident," he says, " that this" (the place to which our Lord descended) " must be some place below the surface of the earth; " for it is said that he ' descended,' that is, he went " down to it. Our Lord's death took place upon the " surface of the earth, where the human race inhabit; " that, therefore, and none higher, is the place from " which he descended; of consequence, the place to " which he went by descent was below it; and it is " with relation to these parts below the surface, that his " rising to life on the third day must be understood. " This was only a return from the nether regions to

" the realms of life and day, from which he had de-
" scended,—not his ascension into heaven, which was
" a subsequent event, and makes a distinct article in
" the Creed."

" The sacred writers of the Old Testament speak
" of such a common mansion in the inner parts of the
" earth: and we find the same opinion so general among
" the heathen writers of antiquity, that it is more pro-
" bable that it had its rise in the earliest patriarchal
" revelations, than in the imaginations of men, or in
" poetical fiction.   The notion is confirmed by the
" language of the writers of the New Testament, with
" this additional circumstance, that they divided this
" central mansion of the dead into two distinct regions,
" for the separate lodging of the souls of the righteous
" and the reprobate.   In this, too, they have the con-
" currence of the earliest heathen poets, who placed the
" good and the bad in separate divisions of the central
" region."*

In respect to the *situation* of Heaven and of Hades,
Dr. Campbell supposes that the " expressions implying
" that *Hades* is *under the earth*, and that the seat of the
" blessed is above the stars, ought to be regarded
" merely as attempts to accommodate what is spoken to
" vulgar apprehensions and language."†

Of the same opinion is Bishop Lowth, who remarks,
—" Observing that after death the body returned to
" the earth, and that it was deposited in a sepulchre
" after the manner which has just been described, a

* Ser. xx. vol. ii.   † Prelim. Diss. vi. part ii.

" sort of popular notion prevailed among the Hebrews,
" as well as among other nations, that the *life which*
" *succeeded the present was to be passed beneath the*
" *earth :* and to this notion even the sacred prophets
" were obliged to allude occasionally, if they wished to
" be understood by the people on this subject."*

From this popular opinion, that the receptacles of
departed souls were under the earth, arose the use of
the word *descended*, in reference to the passage of Christ
into the place of departed spirits.

But though with regard to the *situation* of the receptacle of the departed, there may have been an accommodation to popular notions by the inspired writers,
we shall pervert entirely their meaning, and indeed
render it wholly uncertain, if we suppose that this
accommodation extended to all which they declare
concerning the state of the dead. The basis of popular
fiction in theology is, some truth or fact, which imagination or superstition may embellish or corrupt, but not
to such a degree as to disguise it from the judicious
and discriminating inquirer. And on this principle,
the truths of revelation may be confirmed, by ascertain-
ing the prevalence of opinions allied to them, in the
mythology of Heathen nations. Thus, in the subject
under discussion, the correspondence in many respects
between the theology of the Pagans and that of the
Jews concerning the state of the departed, corroborates
the opinion that both must have had their origin in a

* Lowth on Hebrew Poetry, vol. i. p. 163.

patriarchal revelation; and therefore, divested of the
fictions of imagination, and the corruptions of superstition, must, in essential points, be true.

Whatever be the precise *situation* of the place of
departed spirits, there can be no doubt, considering it
as the *general receptacle* of the souls of the *righteous*
and of the *wicked*, that they exist there in *different
conditions;* and in *different regions* of that unknown
abode; the one in a state of *happiness*, and the other
of *misery*.

Although the *general name* for the receptacle of the
departed, without *particular* reference to their state of
happiness or misery, among the Jews was שאול, *Sheol;*
among the Greeks, ἅδης, *Hades ;* and among the Latins,
Orcus and *Inferi*, all answering to the English word
Hell; they all assigned different abodes in this vast
region, to the righteous and the wicked.

The *Hades* or *Hell* of the Heathen contained the
souls of the *departed*, both good and bad. In his
descent into Hades, Hell, Ulysses not only saw the soul
of Achilles " γηθοσύνη," joyful, traversing the " ἀσφοδιλὺ
" λειμῶνα;" corresponding with the "amena vireta,"
the *flowery plains* of Virgil; but other souls

> "———— ἀχνύμεναι, ειροντο δὲ κηδὶ, ἱκάστη·"
> " All wailing with unutterable woes."*

Æneas, and the Sybil his companion, traverse the
abodes of the departed—

* Homer's Odyss. xi. 536, &c.

" Perque domos Ditis vacuas, et inania regna."*

" ———— the dismal gloom they pass, and tread
" Grim Pluto's courts, the regions of the dead."

Here they view the *different habitations* of the wicked
and the good—
   The gloomy *Tartarus*

   " The seat of night profound, and punished fiends."†

And the fields of *Elysium*

   " ———————— the flowery plains,
   " The verdant groves where endless pleasure reigns."‡

The *Hell* of the Jews seems also to have been distinguished into *two regions*, an upper and a lower Hell,
answering to the *Elysium* and the *Tartarus* of the
poets; the lower Hell being the place destined for the
souls of the wicked. " Thou hast delivered my soul,"
saith the Psalmist, " from the lowest Hell;" on which
passage, St. Austin, in his Commentary, observes—
" We understand it, as if there were two Hells, an
" upper and a lower." Moses describes the justice of
God, (Deut. xxxii. 22,) "a fire is kindled in mine
" anger, and it shall burn unto the lowest Hell,"
(Sheol.)
   There is an ingenious conjecture of Peters, in his.

* Virg. Æn. vi. 269.   † Virg. Æn. vi. 542.
          ‡ Virg. Æn. vi. 638.

" Critical Dissertation on the book of Job,"* that the place for good souls is denoted in the Old Testament, by the phrase which so frequently occurs, of " being " gathered to their fathers," or " their people ;" " to " the assembly of good and pious souls, worshippers " of the true God, who were admitted into covenant " with him, and lived and died in the observance of " that covenant; as the old patriarchs, the ancestors of " the Jewish people, did."†

But the views of the Jews, with respect to a future state, were *comparatively* obscure, because of the imperfection of their dispensation, which was only a " shadow of good things to come."

Agreeably, however, to the representation of the *place of the departed* of the Jews, as consisting of two great divisions for the righteous and wicked, is the account of *Hades* or *Hell* which is given in the New Testament.

Though in the parable of the rich man and Lazarus, every circumstance is not to be understood *literally*, yet the general design of the parable certainly is to show what becomes of the souls of the righteous and the wicked after death. Hell is there represented as a vast region, which, as the receptacle of departed spirits in general, contained the soul of Lazarus in Abraham's bosom, that is, " gathered to his fathers," in a state of blessedness with the father of the faithful; and the soul of Dives in torment in Hell, in the lower Sheol. But

---

* This work is quoted with respect by Archbishop Magee, in his Discourses on the Atonement, note, p. 347.

† Peters' Dissertations on Job, p. 381, 382.

in this immeasurable region, the two abodes of the
righteous and the wicked are " afar off," and between
them is " a great" and impassable " gulf fixed."
There appears a correspondence between this representation and the Pagan notion of the ἅδης, Hades, or
Inferi, the abodes of the departed.   Homer describes
Tartarus, or the place of punishment of the wicked, *as
far* remote from Elysium, both which he comprehends
under the general name of ἄιδης.*

But notwithstanding the distance between these separate regions, and his application of the general term
Hades, to the dwelling of spirits not in punishment, he
seems to consider them as parts of the same region of
the departed.†

So Virgil describes Tartarus as a separate part of the
great region of Orcus, Hell :—

" Respecit Æneas subito ; et subrupe sinistra
" Mænia lata videt, triplici circumdata muro ;
" Quæ rapidus flammis ambit torrentibus amnis
" Tartareus Phlegeton, torquetque sonantia saxa."‡

" The hero, looking on the left, espy'd
" A lofty tower, and strong on every side
" With treble walls which Phlegeton surrounds ;
" Whose fiery flood the burning empire bounds,
" And press'd betwixt the rocks, the bellowing noise resounds."

The accordance between the Hell, or place of the
departed, of the heathen poets, and that of the Jews ;

---

* Illiad viii. 19.   † Odyss. x.
  ‡ Virg. Æn. vi. 548.

and the division of it into two separate abodes for the souls of the righteous and the wicked, are thus clearly established by Dr. Campbell, in the explanation of the parable of the rich man and Lazarus.

" The Jews did not indeed adopt the Pagan fables
" on this subject, nor did they express themselves en-
" tirely in the same manner ; but the general train of
" thinking in both came pretty much to coincide. The
" Greek *Hades* they found well adapted to express the
" Hebrew *Sheol.* This they came to conceive as in-
" cluding different sorts of habitations for ghosts of
" different characters.   And though they did not re-
" ceive the terms *Elysium* or *Elysian fields*, as suit-
" able appellations for the regions peopled by good
" spirits, they took instead of them, as better adapted
" to their own theology, *the garden of Eden* or *Para-
" dise*, a name originally Persian, by which the word
" answering to *garden*, especially when applied to
" Eden, had commonly been rendered by the Seventy.
" To denote the same state, they sometimes used the
" phrase *Abraham's bosom*, a metaphor borrowed from
" the manner in which they reclined at meals. But, on
" the other hand, to express the unhappy situation of
" the wicked in that intermediate state, they do not
" seem to have declined the use of the word *Tartarus.*
" The Apostle Peter says,* of evil angels, that *God
" cast them down to Hell, and delivered them into chains
" of darkness, to be reserved unto judgment.* So it
" stands in the common version, though neither γίεννα

" nor ᾅδης are in the original, where the expression is,
" σειραῖς ζόφου ταρταρώσας παρέδωκεν εἰς κρίσιν τετηρεμένους.
" The word is not γέεννα; for that comes after judg-
" ment, but ταρταρος, which is, as it were, the prison of
" Hades, wherein criminals are kept till the general
" judgment. And as in the ordinary use of the Greek
" word, it was comprehended under *Hades*, as a part;
" it ought, unless we had some positive reason to the
" contrary, by the ordinary rules of interpretation, to
" be understood so here. There is then no inconsist-
" ency in maintaining that the rich man, though in tor-
" ments, was not in *Gehenna*, but in that part of *Hades*
" called *Tartarus*, where we have seen already that
" spirits reserved for judgment are detained in dark-
" ness."

" According to this explication, the rich man and
" Lazarus were both in *Hades*, though in very different
" situations; the latter in the mansions of the happy, and
" the former in those of the wretched. Let us see
" how the circumstances mentioned, and the expres-
" sions used in the parable, will suit this hypothesis.
" First, though they are said to be at a great distance
" from each other, they are still within sight and hear-
" ing. This would have been too gross a violation of
" probability, if the one were considered as inhabiting
" the highest heavens, and the other as placed in the
" infernal regions. Again, the expressions used, are
" such as entirely suit this explanation, and no other;
" for, first, the distance from each other is mentioned,
" but no hint that the one was higher in situation than
" the other; secondly, the terms, whereby motion from

" the one to the other is expressed, are such as are
" never employed in expressing motion to or from Hea-
" ven, but, always, when the places are on a level, or
" nearly so. Thus Lazarus, when dead, is said,*
" ἀπενεχθῆναι, *to be carried away,* not ἀνενεχῆναι, *to be
" carried up,* by angels into Abraham's bosom; where-
" as, it is the latter of these, or one similarly com-
" pounded, that is always used, where an assumption
" into Heaven is spoken of. Thus, the same writer,
" in speaking of our Lord's ascension, says,† ἀνεφέρετο
" εἰς τον οὐρανον; and Mark, in relation to the event, says,‡
" ἀνελήφθη εἰς τον οὐρανον, *he was taken up into Heaven.*
" These words are also used, wherever one is said to
" be conveyed from a lower to a higher situation. But
" what is still more decisive in this way; where men-
" tion is made of passing from Abraham to the rich
" man, and inversely, the verbs employed are, διαβαίνω
" and διαπεράω, words which always denote motion on
" the same ground or level; as, passing a river or lake,
" passing through the Red Sea, or passing from Asia
" to Macedonia. But, when Heaven is spoken of as
" the termination to which, or from which the pas-
" sage is made, the word is invariably either in the
" first case, ἀναβαίνω, and in the second, καταβαίνω, or
" some word similarly formed, and of the same import.
" Thus, both the circumstances of the story, and the
" expressions employed in it, confirm the explanation
" I have given. For if the sacred penmen wrote to be
" understood, they must have employed their words

---

*Luke xvi. 22.   † Luke xxiv. 51.   ‡ Mark xvi. 19.

" and phrases in conformity to the current usage of
" those for whom they wrote."

That region of the departed, where the souls of the
righteous repose, in the interval between death and the
resurrection, is denominated by our Saviour *Paradise.*
" This day," says he to the penitent thief, " thou shalt
" be with me in Paradise;" not in *Heaven*, the region
of the blessed. For, as Bishop Horsley observes*—
" Paradise was certainly some place where our Lord
" was to be on the very day on which he suffered, and
" where the companion of his sufferings was to be with
" him. It was not Heaven; for to Heaven our Lord
" ascended not till after his resurrection, as appears
" from his own words to Mary Magdalen. He was not
" therefore in Heaven on the day of the crucifixion;
" and, where *he* was not, the thief could not be with
" him. It was no place of torment, for to any such
" place the name of Paradise never was applied. It
" could be no other than the region of repose and rest,
" where the souls of the righteous abide in joyful hope
" of the consummation of their bliss."

" Paradise, among the Jews"—observes Bishop
Bull—" primarily signified *the garden of Eden*, that
" blessed garden wherein Adam in his state of inno-
" cence dwelt. By which, because it was a most plea-
" sant and delightful place, they were wont symboli-
" cally to represent the place and state of good souls
" separated from their bodies, and waiting for the re-
" surrection; whom they believed to be in a state of

* Sermons, vol. ii. 92.

" happiness far exceeding all the felicities of this life ;
" but yet inferior to tnat consummate bliss which fol-
" lows the resurrection. Hence it was the solemn good
" wish of the Jews (as the learned tell us from the
" Talmudists) concerning their dead friend, *Let his*
" *soul be in the garden of Eden,* or, *Let his soul be*
" *gathered into the garden of Eden.* And in their
" prayers for a dying person, they used to say, *Let him*
" *have his portion in Paradise, and also in the world to*
" *come.* In which form *Paradise, and the world to*
" *come,* are plainly distinguished. According to which
" notion, the meaning of our Saviour, in his promise
" to the penitent thief, is evidently this—that he should
" presently after his death enter with him into that place
" of bliss and happiness, where the souls of the righte-
" ous, separated from their bodies, inhabit, and where
" they wait in a joyful expectation of the resurrection,
" and the consummation of their bliss in the highest
" Heaven. For that our Saviour here did not promise
" the thief an immediate entrance into that Heaven, the
" ancients gathered from hence, that he himself, as
" man, did not ascend thither till after his resurrection,
" as our very Creed informs us ; which is also St. Aus-
" tin's argument in his fifty-seventh epistle."

Dr. Adam Clarke observes, in his Commentary,
that " the garden of Eden, mentioned Gen. ii. 8, is
" also called from the Septuagint, the *garden of Para-*
" *dise.* Hence the word has been transplanted into
" the New Testament, and is used to signify a place of
" exquisite delight. The word Paradise is not Greek,
" but is of Asiatic origin. In Arabic and Persian,

" it signifies a *garden*, a *vineyard*, the *place of the*
" *blessed.* Our Lord's words intimate that this peni-
" tent should be immediately taken to the *abode of the*
" *spirits of the just*, where they should enjoy the pre-
" sence and approbation of the Most High."*

Dr. Whitby considers Paradise as " the place into
" which pious souls, *separated from the body*, were im-
" mediately received."†

Dr. Doddridge also speaks of Paradise as " the
" abode of happy spirits when *separate* from the body,‡
" that garden of God which is the seat of happy spirits
" in the *intermediate state*, and during their separation
" from the body."

Now, as in Heaven, happy spirits are *united with
their glorified bodies*, the place where they abide, when
separate from their bodies, is not Heaven, but a region
of the place of the departed, styled *Paradise.*

Dr. Macknight states,§ that " the name *Paradise*
" was also given to the place where the spirits of the
" just, after death, reside in felicity till the resurrection;
" as appears from our Lord's words to the penitent
" thief."

It may be asked—is not this view of Paradise, as a
place of *enjoyment* to the righteous, and yet a part of
Hades or Hell, incompatible with the figurative representation of this latter place as an enemy which Christ
is to conquer, and from whose power he is to redeem
his people ?—" I will redeem them from the power of

---

* Clarke's Com. on Luke xxiii. 43.   † Whitby on Luke xxiii. 43.
‡ Doddridge on Luke xxiii. 43.   § Com. on 2 Cor. xii. 4.

" the grave," *(Sheol* or Hell,) Hosea xiii. 14. Bishop
Horsley answers this inquiry—" The state of the de-
" parted saints, while they continue there," (in Sheol,
Hades, Hell, the place of the departed,) " is a condi-
" tion of unfinished bliss, in which the souls of the
" justified would not have remained for any time, (if
" indeed they had ever entered it,) had not sin intro-
" duced death.   It is a state, therefore, consequent
" upon death ; consequent, therefore, upon sin, though
" no part of the punishment of it.   And the resurrec-
" tion of the saints is often described as an enlargement
" of them by our Lord's power, from confinement in a
" place, not of punishment, but of inchoate enjoyment
" only.   ' Our Lord will break the gates of brass, and
" cut the bars of iron in sunder,' and set at liberty ' his
" prisoners of hope.' And when this place of safe keep-
" ing is personified, it is, consistently with these no-
" tions of it, represented as one of the enemies which
" Christ is to subdue."

Against the opinion, that Paradise is a distinct place
from Heaven, it may be urged, that St. Paul speaks*
of " being caught up into the third *Heavens*," and
" being caught up into *Paradise.*" It was the opinion
of all the ancient Fathers that St. Paul speaks of two
distinct visions, and of course the scenes of these visions, the third Heavens and Paradise, are not neces-
sarily the same. Dr. Whitby maintains that there were
different visions, and that *Paradise* is *distinct* from the
third *Heavens*.   " The opinion of all the ancients," he

* 2 Cor, xii. 1—4.

observes, " seems to have been this, that he was caught
" at *several times* into *several places*. Hence it doth
" not follow that Paradise is in the third Heaven."*

The learned Bishop Bull makes the same distinction between the visions of St. Paul, and between *Paradise* and the *third Heavens;*† in which he is followed
by Dr. Doddridge.‡ And Dr. Campbell establishes
this distinction, in the Preliminary Dissertation which
has been so often quoted. The phrase, being *caught
up*, may be supposed contrary to the usual phraseology
of Scripture, with respect to Hades or Paradise. But,
as Campbell observes, the phrase αρπάζω expresses
more the suddenness of the event, and the passiveness
of the Apostle, than the direction of the motion.

The phrase, " Paradise of God," may seem to denote Heaven in Rev. ii. 7—" To him that overcometh
" will I give to eat of the tree of life, which is in the
" midst of the Paradise of God." " Here," as Dr.
Campbell observes, " our Lord, no doubt, speaks of
" Heaven ; but as he plainly alludes to the state of mat-
" ters in the garden of Eden, where our first parents
" were placed, and where the tree of life grew, it can
" only be understood as *a figurative expression of the*

* Whitby on 2 Cor. xii. 1—4.
† Bishop Bull's Sermons, vol. i. 89, 97.
‡ Com. on 2 Cor. xii. 1—4. Dr. *Macknight*, and Dr. *Adam
Clarke*, are favourable to the same opinion; from which *Scott*
differs, because, he says, the happiness of departed saints consists
in being present with the Lord. As if God's blissful presence
could not be in Paradise as well as in Heaven.

" *promise of eternal life*, forfeited by Adam, but re-
" covered by our Lord Jesus Christ."

Thus, then, it appears, from the above view, that
the *Sheol* of the Old Testament, and the ἄδης, or *Hell*,
of the New, means the place of departed spirits, where
the *souls* of the righteous and the wicked abide, in separate states of happiness or misery, until the day of
judgment; and that into the division of this region
called Paradise, the abode of the spirits of the righteous, the soul of our Saviour went after his death.

The ends of our Saviour's descent, into the place
of the departed, were of the most important nature.

1. In this respect, as in all others, he was made like
unto us.   The separation of the body from the soul by
death, the penalty of Adam's sin, he, as the second
Adam, underwent.   His body was deposited in the
grave, where our bodies must slumber.   And to complete his conformity to us, his soul went to that place
of the departed, where our souls are to abide during
their absence from the body.   This conformity, in all
respects to us, sin only excepted, was a part of that
humiliation by which he sustained the penalties of our
transgressions.

2. And thus, as our Redeemer and Head, sanctify-
ing by his presence the place of the departed, he hath
divested this secret and retired abode of its terrors, and
enlightened it by his mercy and grace.   The πύλαι ἄδυ,

the *gates of Hades* he hath opened; and by his power they become, to the faithful, the entrance to a joyful re-surrection of life and glory.

3. To afford us a pledge of this victory not only over death, but over Hades, over Hell, the place that confines our spirits during their separation from the body, was the last great object of his descent into it. " In Hell, in Hades, his soul was not left." Neither shall the souls of his people there remain. " He " opened the gates of brass; he burst asunder the bars " of iron;" and his spirit, disengaged from its prison-house, and united to his body, ascended in glory to the regions of heavenly light. And when he who still holds the keys of Hell, of this invisible receptacle of the departed, shall pronounce the sentence, " Go forth," the souls of his redeemed shall ascend, in the vest-ments of a glorified and incorruptible body, to that Heaven where there is " fulness of joy."

The fact that Christ, in the interval between his death and his resurrection, went into the *place of departed spirits,* being proved, the existence of this place is of course established.

With regard to the position, in proof of the exist-ence of the place of the departed, that an appropriate term, ἅδης, answering to the Hebrew *SHEOL,* and to the original meaning of the word Hell, as a *secret* or *invisible* place, is uniformly applied, in the New Tes-tament, to this state of departed spirits; it may be sa- .

tisfactory to review all the passages of the New Testament where the word ᾅδης, Hades, occurs.

The word ᾅδης, Hades, is found only in eleven places, and in all of them it denotes the *place of departed spirits.*

1. It occurs Acts ii. 27, and

2. Also Acts ii. 31, as applicable to our Saviour's soul being in Hell; the meaning of which, as denoting the place of departed spirits, has been, in the preceding pages, fully considered.

3. Luke xvi. 23. It occurs in the parable of the rich man and Lazarus, in the same signification. See p. 74.

4. Matt. xi. 23—" And thou Capernaum, which art " exalted to Heaven, shall be cast down to Hell," (ἕως ᾅδου.)
Heaven and Hell, or Hades, are here figuratively used; Heaven denoting the highest object, and Hell or Hades the lowest, according to the notions of the Jews and Pagans in regard to the situation of these places. Capernaum being exalted to Heaven denotes her *flourishing state,* and brought down to Hell, her *low* or *depressed* condition; even a state in which she would be no more *seen;* alluding to the signification of Hades, as an invisible place. Whitby, Doddridge, Schleusner, and Clarke, agree in this construction of the passage.

5. The words occur in the same sense and application in Luke x. 15.

6. Matt. xvi. 18—" The gates of Hell (πύλαι ἅδε,
" the gates of Hades) shall not prevail against it," the
Church. The expression is here figurative. Hades,
or the place of the dead, is represented as a spacious
receptacle with gates, through which the dead enter.
Hezekiah speaks (Isa. xxxviii. 10,) of the *gates of*
the grave or Hades, and Homer speaks of Achilles
hating (ἀΐδας πύλησιν,) " as the gates of Hell or Hades,"
that is, hating mortally.* The expression, then, " the
" gates of Hell" (Hades) " shall not prevail against the
" Church," means, it shall never enter the place of the
departed, it shall *never die*, it shall *continue for ever*.

" The full meaning of this promise of our Lord,"
says Parkhurst,† " seems to be that his Church on
" earth, however persecuted and distressed, *should*
" *never fail* till the consummation of all things, and
" should then, at the resurrection of the just, finally
" triumph over death and the grave." Dr. Doddridge
gives the same construction to this passage, and ob-
serves‡—" It is most certain that the phrase πύλαι ἅδε,
" does generally, in the Greek writers, signify the *en-*
" *trance* into the *invisible world*." Dr. Campbell, in
his Preliminary Dissertation, and Dr. Whitby, on this
text, prove, at great length, that the expression, the

---

* Iliad ix. 312.   † Parkhurst, Article ἅδης.
‡ Com. on this text.

gates of Hades, denotes, both among Jewish and Christian writers, the *invisible world:* and they establish the above construction of this text.

7. 1 Cor. xv. 55—"O grave (in the margin, Hell, "original ᾅδη) where is thy victory." The place of separate spirits is here meant, from which, at the resurrection at the last day, the spirits of the departed shall come forth, to be "clothed upon with their house "that is from Heaven." There seems to be here an allusion to Hosea xii. 13, which Bishop Horsley translates—"Death! I will be thy pestilence. Hell! I "will be thy burning plague"—on which he has the following note—"Hell, not the place where the damned "are to suffer their torment, but the invisible place, "where the souls of the departed remain till the ap- "pointed time shall come for the reunion of soul and "body." The Hebrew word Sheol, answering to the Greek Hades, is here improperly translated *grave,* which is denoted in the Hebrew by a distinct word, KEBER. "No two things"—Bishop Horsley observes—"can be more distinct; *Hell* is the mansion of "the departed spirit; the *grave* is the receptacle of the "dead body."*

8. Rev. i. 18—"I have the keys of Hell (τȣ ᾅδȣ) "and of death." The Lord Jesus Christ is here represented as not only having power over death, to redeem the *body* from its dominion, but as holding the

* Com. on Hosea, p. 159.

keys of *Hell*, of the place of the departed, from which
he will release them, and reunite them to their incorruptible bodies. Dr. Doddridge, on this text, paraphrases *Hell* as the *unseen world*, the invisible state in
which the souls of men remain until Christ exerts his
power of raising the dead.* The notions of Scott, in
his Commentary, with respect to this subject, seem
somewhat confused and contradictory. On this text,
however, he unequivocally acknowledges a distinct
state of departed spirits. His words are as follows—
" He (the Lord Jesus Christ) possesses the absolute
" sovereignty, as dwelling in human nature, over the
" invisible world, the *state of separate spirits*, and
" over death and the grave, so that he removes men
" out of this life, and consigns their bodies to the
" grave and corruption, when, and as he pleases; he
" then fixes their *souls* in *happiness* or *misery* with ab-
" solute authority; and he will soon *raise* all their *dead*
" *bodies*, and either receive them into *Heaven*, or shut
" them up for ever in *Hell*, as he sees good." In this
passage, there is the *state of separate spirits*, in which
the souls of men are either in happiness or misery,
until their dead bodies being raised and united to their
souls, they are fixed in the final *Heaven* of happiness,
and *Hell* of torments.

9. Rev. vi. 8—" And I looked, and behold a pale
" horse, and his name that sat on him was Death, and
" Hell (ᾅδης) followed with him."

***

* See Doddridge's note, on this text, in this Dissertation,

12

10. Rev. xx. 13—" Death and Hell (ᾅδης) delivered
" up the dead that were in them."

11. Rev. xx. 14—" And death and Hell (ᾅδης)
" were cast into the lake of fire. This is the second
" death."

These passages are very bold and sublime personi-
fications.   In the first, *Hell*, the place of departed spirits, follows death, denoting, that immediately after
the body becomes subject to the dominion of death,
Hell or the invisible place receives the soul.

But, as is declared in the second passage, *death* shall
deliver up the bodies, and *Hell* the spirits that were
subject to their dominion.   And,

As is announced in the last verse, death, as well as
Hell, the place of the departed, shall be destroyed,
shall be cast into the lake of fire.   " The *death* which
" consists in the separation of the soul and body, and
" the *state of souls* intervening between death and
" judgment, shall be no more.   To the wicked they
" shall be succeeded by a more terrible death, the
" damnation of *Gehenna*," the *Hell* of torments.

The last passage is an incontrovertible evidence,
that Hell is applied to the place of the departed.   If
by Hell we understand the place of torments; as by
the *lake of fire*, by which the second death is denominated, the Hell of torments is undoubtedly meant;
then the personification becomes absolute nonsense—
the Hell of torments is cast into the Hell of torments.*

---

* See Dr. Campbell's Prelim. Diss. vi. part ii. p. 13.

Dr. Doddridge considers Hell in these passages as denoting the *separate state.* And Dr. Scott again un-equivocally avows its existence. He thus comments on these passages—" The grave and *separate state* will " give up the bodies and souls contained in them." " Then *death* and *Hell,* the *grave* and *separate state,* " (represented as two persons,) will be cast into the " lake of fire : that is, they shall subsist no longer to " *receive the bodies and the souls of men.*"

The only instance of a personification, equal in bold-ness and sublimity to that contained in the above pas-sages, is where the prophet Isaiah represents the de-parted souls of mighty monarchs, in *the place of the departed,* as in motion and agitation at the approach of the departed spirit of the king of Babylon. " Hell " from beneath is moved for thee, to meet thee at thy " coming, it stirreth up the dead for thee."*

The above, it is believed, are all the passages in the New Testament in which the English word *Hell* is found corresponding to ᾅδης, Hades, in the original, and denoting the place of the departed.

There are thirteen passages in the New Testament in which the word Hell is found expressed by γέεννα, Gehenna, in the original, and denoting the place of torment.

A summary of this doctrine of a *place of departed spirits* may be thus exhibited.

---

* Isaiah xiv. 9.

As the souls of men are not admitted into Heaven, the place of final happiness; nor into Hell, the place of final torment; according to the representations of the sacred writings, until the resurrection, and the judgment of the great day; and as the soul, both from reason and Scripture, is not previously in a state of unconsciousness,* it follows, that during this interval, she must subsist in a *separate state.*

As the happiness of Heaven, and the misery of Hell, the place of final torment, are represented in Scripture as the happiness or misery of the *whole man*, of his body united to his soul; and as this union, dissolved by death, is not renewed until the resurrection and judgment of the great day; it follows, that previously to this event, the soul cannot be a subject of the happiness of Heaven, or of the misery of the final Hell of torment, but must be in a *separate* state of incomplete, though inconceivably great felicity or woe.

And that there is this place of the departed, denominated, in allusion to its secret and invisible character, ᾅδης, Hades or Hell, where, in *distinct* abodes, the souls of the righteous and of the wicked experience inconceivable happiness or misery, expecting the consummation of their felicity or woe, at the day of judgment, is placed beyond doubt by the fact that Christ's human soul was in Hell, (Hades,) in the place of the

* In the Dissertation, I have not repeated the arguments in favour of the conscious state of the soul when separated by death from the body, which are succinctly stated in the Address.

departed, and in that part of this place denominated Paradise, in the interval between his death and his resurrection. For,

During this interval, his human soul was in some place: since, independently of every other consideration, it was declared of him by the prophet, that " his " soul was not to be *left* in Hell."

But his soul, during this period, could not have been in Heaven; for he did not ascend to Heaven, agreeably to his own declaration, until after his resurrection.

Nor could his soul have been in the Hell of torment, (an impious supposition,) for he declared, as matter of triumph and joy to the penitent thief, that after death they should be together in Paradise.

In Paradise, then, that region of peace and joy, in Hades, the place of the departed, was the human soul of the blessed Jesus in the interval between death and the resurrection.

And where the human soul of Jesus was during this period, there, during the same period, must be the souls of the human race whose sentence of mortality he sustained, and of whom he was the representative.

This doctrine has not the most remote connection with the *papal* doctrine of *purgatory.*

That the celebrated Protestants whose names have been exhibited in support of this doctrine, in the preceding pages; that Campbell, and Doddridge, and Macknight, Presbyterian divines; that Bishops Taylor, Bull, Burnet, Secker, Horsley, Tomline, and other

Bishops of the English Church ; that Hammond, and Whitby, and Clarke, and Scott, clergymen, and Sir Peter King, a distinguished layman of that Church ; that Wesley, and Clarke, of the Methodist communion ; that Bishops Seabury, and White, of our own Church ; that all these, living in different ages and countries, and of different religious denominations, should have conspired to introduce the papal doctrine of purgatory, will hardly be credited.

The papal doctrine is, that " some few have before " their death so fully cleared up their accounts with " the Divine Majesty, and washed away all their stains " in the blood of the Lamb, as to go straight to Hea- " ven after death ; and that others who die in the guilt " of deadly sins, go straight to Hell."* The doctrine set forth in the preceding pages is, that none go to Heaven, or to Hell, (γίεννα, Gehenna,) until after the day of judgment. In the interval between death and the resurrection, they are in a state of unchangeable happiness or misery in the place of the departed.

The papal doctrine is, that those who do not die perfectly pure and clean, nor yet under the guilt of unrepented deadly sin, go to purgatory, where they suffer certain indefinable pains, and the pains of material fire, until God's justice is satisfied, or they are freed from these pains by the masses said for their souls. These

* The Catholic Christian Instructed, p. 176—a book of standard authority among the Roman Catholics, published by one of their distinguished Bishops, the Right Rev. Dr. Chaloner.

tenets, it must be apparent, are in no degree sanctioned by the doctrine advanced in the preceding pages, with respect to departed spirits. The eternal destiny of the individual is unchangeably fixed at death. His condition, in the place of the departed, is an *unchangeable* condition of happiness or misery, until the day of judgment, when this happiness or misery is consummated in body and soul.

The papal doctrine with respect to Christ's descent into Hell is, that he went not into the place of departed spirits, as is believed by those who maintain the existence of this place, but into a region called *Limbus Patrum,* to manifest his glory to the holy saints, who had departed before his advent, and to release them from their confinement, and take them to Heaven.

There is thus a total dissimilarity between the papal doctrine of purgatory and the doctrine of the descent into Hell, and the state of the departed, advanced in the preceding pages.

The sermon of Bishop Bull, (from which Dr. Doddridge quotes with approbation,*) in which he establishes this doctrine of a place of departed spirits, contains a refutation of the papal doctrine of purgatory, and shows the entire difference between it and the doctrine which he advocates of an intermediate state. After exhibiting the faith of the primitive Church on

* See page 59.

this point, he observes*—" From what hath been said,
" it appears that the doctrine of the distinction of the
" joys of Paradise, the portion of good souls in that
" state of separation, from that yet fuller and most
" complete beatitude of the kingdom of Heaven, after
" the resurrection, consisting in that clearest vision of
" God, which the Holy Scriptures call seeing him *face
" to face*, is far from being popery, as some have
" ignorantly censured it ; for we see it was the current
" doctrine of the first and purest ages of the Church.
" I add, that it is so far from being popery, that it is
" directly the contrary. For it was the popish conven-
" tion at *Florence*,† that first boldly defined against the
" sense of the primitive Christians—*That those souls,
" which having contracted the blemish of sin, are, ei-
" ther in their bodies or out of them, purged from it,
" do presently go into Heaven, and there clearly behold
" God himself, one God in three Persons, as he is.*
" And this decree they made, partly to establish their
" superstition of prayer to the saints deceased, whom
" they would needs make us believe, to see and know
" all our necessities and concerns *in speculo Trinitatis,
" in the glass of the Trinity*, as they call it, and so to
" be fit objects of our religious invocation ; but chiefly
" to introduce their purgatory, and that the prayers of
" the ancient Church for the dead might be thought to
" be founded on a supposition, that the souls of some
" faithful persons after death go into a place of grievous
" torment."

---

* Bull's Ser. vol. i. p. 114.   † In the 15th Century.

This doctrine of the separate existence of the soul, in the place of the departed, between death and the resurrection, being expressly revealed, should be an object of faith.

1. It resolves all doubts with repect to the condition of the soul after her departure from the body, and before her reunion to it at the resurrection. The soul, during this period, is in a state of consciousness; either enjoying a foretaste of future bliss, or tormented by the anticipated pangs of future woe, after the judgment of the great day.

2. It is thus calculated to fill the wicked with dismay. It cuts off the hope of a moment's intermission of torment after death. The worm that never dies immediately begins to gnaw. In the company of spirits, wretched like themselves, they dwell in the dark region of the departed, anticipating the summons which, uniting them to incorruptible bodies, will bring them to the judgment-seat, and also the more dread sentence that will consign them to *Gehenna*, to the Hell of torment, the " lake of fire" that " burneth for ever and ever."

3. But this doctrine of the place of the departed is full of consolation to the faithful disciples of the Lord Jesus. It assures them that, in the long interval between death and the resurrection, while detained from Heaven, they shall not be deprived of a foretaste of its glories. In the bosom of Abraham, in the enjoyment of his society, and of the blessed fellowship of all the

departed saints, they shall experience the most exalted delights. "Delivered from the burden of the flesh," their souls shall be with the Lord Jesus, the rays of whose glory sanctify and cheer the *Paradise* of his saints. Here they shall enjoy perpetual peace and felicity; anticipating their " consummation both in body " and soul in God's eternal and everlasting glory."

Why, then, Christian, shouldest thou fear to die? Thy soul is not, for a moment, to lose that consciousness which is dear to her as her existence. The darkness of death is not, for a moment, to cover thy spirit. The instant thou dost close thine eyes on the world, thy soul opens her joyful vision on the delights of Paradise. And Paradise is but the introduction to that *Heaven*, where, thy *whole nature* perfected and glorified, thou shalt taste the fulness of joy, and " be for " ever with the Lord."

THE END.

BOOKS

Published by T. & J. Swords, No. 99 Pearl-street.

The Holy Bible, including the Old and New Testaments, and the Apocrypha, according to the authorized Version; with Notes, Explanatory and Practical; taken principally from the most eminent writers of the United Church of England and Ireland; together with appropriate Introductions, Tables, and Indexes. Prepared and arranged by the Rev. George D'Oyly, B. D. and the Rev. Richard Mant, D. D. Domestic Chaplains to his Grace the Lord Archbishop of Canterbury. Under the direction of the Society for Promoting Christian Knowledge. For the Use of Families. The first American edition, with additional Notes, selected and arranged by John Henry Hobart, D. D. Bishop of the Protestant Episcopal Church in the State of New-York.

Sermons on the Principal Events and Truths of Redemption. By John Henry Hobart, D. D. Bishop of the Protestant Episcopal Church in the State of New-York. In 2 vols. 8vo.

A Companion for the Festivals and Fasts of the Protestant Episcopal Church in the United States of America. Principally selected and altered from Nelson's Companion for the Festivals and Fasts of the Church of England. With Forms of Devotion. By John Henry Hobart, D. D. Bishop of the Protestant Episcopal Church in the State of New-York.

A Companion for the Altar; or Week's Preparation for the Holy Communion. Consisting of a short Explanation of the Lord's Supper, and Meditations and Prayers, proper to be used before, and during, the receiving of the Holy Communion, according to the Form prescribed by the Protestant Episcopal Church in the United States of America. By John Henry Hobart, D. D. Bishop of the Protestant Episcopal Church in the State of New-York.

The Clergyman's Companion, containing the occasional Offices of the Protestant Episcopal Church, used by the Clergy of the said Church in the Discharge of their Parochial Duties. To which are added, Extracts from the Writings of distinguished Divines on the Qualifications and Duties of the Clerical Office.

The Christian's Manual of Faith and Devotion : containing Dialogues and Prayers suited to the various Exercises of the Christian Life, and an Exhortation to Ejaculatory Prayer, with Forms of Ejaculatory and other Prayers. The second edition improved. To which are added, a number of additional Prayers.

An Apology for Apostolic Order and its Advocates, occasioned by the Strictures and Denunciations of the Christian's Magazine. In a Series of Letters, addressed to the Rev. John M. Mason, D. D. the Editor of that Work. By the Rev. John Henry Hobart, an Assistant Minister of Trinity Church.

Sermons, by Benjamin Moore, D. D. late Bishop of the Protestant Episcopal Church in the State of New-York. In 2 vols. 8vo.

The Life of Samuel Johnson, D. D. the first President of King's College, in New-York. Containing many interesting Anecdotes; a general View of the State of Religion and Learning in Connecticut during the former Part of the last Century; and an Account of the Institution and Rise of Yale College, Connecticut; and of King's (now Columbia) College, New-York. By Thomas Bradbury Chandler, D. D. formerly Rector of St. John's Church, Elizabeth-Town, New-Jersey. To which is added, an Appendix, containing many original Letters, never before published, from Bishop Berkeley, Archbishop Secker, Bishop Lowth, and others, to Dr. Johnson.

www.ingramcontent.com/pod-product-compliance
Lightning Source LLC
Chambersburg PA
CBHW032157010726
47493CB00008BA/2729